Brennan recognized Stella Maxwell from the professional photograph that always accompanied her byline.

That photo didn't do her justice because the young woman was breathtaking in spite of the blood splatter on her clothes. He ignored the fact that she'd been trying to reach him for weeks now, wanting a comment or interview about his progress with finding the Landmark Killer. He had sent her calls to voice mail and her emails to his trash bin. He had neither needed nor wanted any media attention on the serial killer who was proving to be so elusive.

Now, sitting there, she looked frazzled, her teary expression pulling at his heartstrings. He found himself wanting to pull her close, to ease his arms around her torso and comfort her. The rush of emotion was suddenly unsettling, and totally out of his character. Most especially since he had no idea how she was connected to the dead man now lying under a green tarp.

Stella suddenly called his name.

"Agent Brennan Colton? Excuse me! Agent Colton, it's me, Stella Maxwell!"

Dear Reader,

The Colton family is back at it, and this time, the New York branch of the family is keeping you on the edge of your seat! Finding love while fending off the bad guys should come with disclaimers because FBI Agent Brennan Colton and journalist Stella Maxwell burn up the pages from beginning to end. I loved breathing life into this couple. Brennan battles criminals, his own demons and his heart with the conviction of a predator determined not to lose his prey. Stella is a spitfire with take-charge energy, and she readily gives him a run for his money. She is not a woman to be played with and will make a man cry just to start her day. I love both of these characters so much and I hope you will, too!

I am truly honored to be associated with the wonderful authors who comprise the Colton series team. To be included in this authors' club has challenged me to be a better writer with each and every book. I appreciate their kindness and support. Romance authors rock!

Thank you so much for your support. I am always humbled by all the love you keep showing me, my characters and our stories. I know that none of this would be possible without you. If you'd like, you can connect with me at my website, www.deborahmello.org.

Until the next time, please take care and may God's blessings be with you always.

With much love,

Deborah Fletcher Mello

CHASING A COLTON KILLER

Deborah Fletcher Mello

HARLEQUIN
ROMANTIC
SUSPENSE

Special thanks and acknowledgment are given to Deborah Fletcher Mello for her contribution to The Coltons of New York miniseries.

Recycling programs
for this product may
not exist in your area.

ISBN-13: 978-1-335-59370-2

Chasing a Colton Killer

Copyright © 2023 by Harlequin Enterprises ULC

For questions and comments about the quality of this book, please contact us at CustomerService@Harlequin.com.

Harlequin Enterprises ULC
22 Adelaide St. West, 41st Floor
Toronto, Ontario M5H 4E3, Canada
www.Harlequin.com

Printed in U.S.A.

A true Renaissance woman, **Deborah Fletcher Mello** finds joy in crafting unique story lines and memorable characters. She's received accolades from several publications, including *Publishers Weekly, Library Journal* and *RT Book Reviews*. Born and raised in Connecticut, Deborah now considers home to be wherever the moment moves her.

Books by Deborah Fletcher Mello

Harlequin Romantic Suspense

Visit the Author Profile page at Harlequin.com for more titles.

To Carly Silver,

Thank you for trusting me, encouraging me,

and pushing me out of my comfort zone.

I miss working with you.

Chapter 1

The noise in the newsroom of the *New York Wire* rose to stadium-grade level, sounding like the last touchdown cheers of a winning football game. Reporters, editors and photographers were all shouting over one another, each desperate to make a point or get dibs in on a perspective story. It was chaos. Organized chaos but chaos nonetheless.

Stella Maxwell stepped into the space dubbed the "war room," having just left an early morning meeting with the editorial team. It wasn't even eleven o'clock in the morning, and she'd already put in five hours of work. Now her head hurt.

She stared at the computer on her desk. The screen saver was a quote by Joseph Pulitzer that read, "The power to mold the future of the republic will be in the hands of the journalists of future generations."

There was a time she believed that, but with each passing day, she was starting to think that the future lay in the hands of rogue teenagers who trolled the internet, spurned authority and put all their trust in the almighty dollar. She hated teenagers. In fact, she had a strong dislike for most children in general. Most especially since being assigned a story on dangerous TikTok challenges happening in New York City public schools. If the little demons weren't blowing up each other, they were blowing up someone's property.

Stella thought the future looked bleak if left in the hands of younger iGens, who had no boundaries and believed the entire world owed them a pass for simply breathing. Yes, she said it. To herself, of course. Now to figure out how to convey that message in a quarter page piece with her byline and not insult those people who actually liked the little monsters.

Working for the *New York Wire* was not Stella's job du jour. It paid the bills, but truth be told, it left her less than satisfied. Although she loved journalism and put every ounce of herself into all of her assignments, she would have preferred to be writing for the *New York Times* or the *Washington Post*, newspapers with better visibility and more credibility. Publications that were worthy of the substantial talent she brought to the table. She considered her current job a stepping stone to bigger and better, her career of choice eventually netting her Pulitzer gold. She suddenly laughed aloud, drawing looks from the men sitting in the cubicles beside her.

"What's so funny?" Garrett Hoffman asked. He was the pop culture editor, and they often lunched together while bouncing stories off one another.

Stella shook her head. "If I don't laugh, I'm going to cry. It's starting to be that kind of week."

"Can I help?" the young man asked, eyeing her with bright baby blue eyes and thick lashes the color of corn silk.

Shrugging her shoulders, Stella blew a soft sigh. "Just pray for me. I'm headed to PS 41 down in Greenwich Village later today to interview a gang of middle schoolers."

"Have you brushed up on your cool kid jargon so you don't come off old?"

"I am old. I'm about to be thirty, and in their eyes, that's ancient!"

"Exactly, which is why you need to know how to talk their lingo. Otherwise, those little monsters will eat you alive!"

The duo laughed.

"What are you working on?" Stella questioned. She leaned back in her chair, rocking slowly back and forth.

"Waiting for confirmation on a Kim and Kanye reconciliation."

"That will never happen!"

"Says you!"

"And Kim! She's had her rebound fling with Pete What's-his-name, and now she's ready to move on to something more serious. She's not going back to babysit her past mistakes."

"And if she does?"

"You'll be writing another breakup story in six months."

"And people say I need to get my life together." He sighed heavily.

Stella laughed again. The phone on her desk rang, the unexpected chime startling her ever so slightly.

Garrett laughed at her again. "It looks like duty is calling you!"

"With my luck, it'll be a wrong number," Stella said as she reached for the receiver and pulled it to her ear. "Thank you for calling the *Wire*. This is Stella Maxwell."

"There's a man being murdered in the alley behind your building."

Stella bristled. "Excuse me? Who is this?"

"He'll be dead if you don't come now," the caller said. "Can you save him, Stella?"

Stella didn't recognize the voice and found it difficult to distinguish whether it was male or female. There was the faintest hint of digitization, and she knew, whoever the caller was, they were masking their sound with a voice modifier. With the many free apps that could be downloaded and used during gaming or phone calls, they had the ability to make a person sound deeper, higher or even like the opposite sex. For all Stella knew, the caller could have been anyone.

She asked again, the barest hint of anxiety in her

own tone. "Who the hell is this? And why are you calling me?"

"I guess you don't want the story," the caller said, and then they disconnected the line.

Stella stared at the phone receiver for a brief second before dropping it back down on the cradle.

"What's up?" Garrett questioned.

"I'm not sure if I'm being pranked or tossed a story I can scoop," she said as she rose swiftly from her seat, grabbing her purse and her cell phone.

"Where are you going?"

"To check out a tip," she said, hurrying to the elevator. She shouted over her shoulder. "I'll call you later!"

As she rode the elevator down to the first floor, the phone chimed, signaling an incoming text message. The message reiterated what the caller had just told her.

There's a man being murdered in the alley beside your building. Can you save him? Come now or he'll die on your watch, Stella!

Stepping out of the elevator, Stella paused, forwarding the message to a dispatcher friend at the 911 call center. She added the Forty-Seventh Street address and asked her to send a patrol car. Just in case it wasn't a prank.

Dropping her phone back into her handbag, she exited the building, turning toward the corner and the back side of the high-rise office building. People pushed past her, unconcerned as they made their way to their own destinations. It was the city and everyone was in a rush. They ignored her as she ignored them, a single thought on her mind. *Please, God, let this be a prank.*

Rounding the backside of the building, she entered the alley, her eyes skating swiftly back and forth. Her stomach suddenly pitched, her gaze widening as she caught sight of a man lying on the ground, blood beginning to pool beneath his torso. Stella looked around a second time as she inched closer to the body, and then she recognized him, his blue eyes meeting hers. It was Rockwell Henley, the boyfriend who'd dumped her via text message just days earlier.

Stella screamed Rockwell's name as she dropped down beside his body, noting the large butcher knife stuck in his chest. She pulled his head into her lap and cried out for help.

FBI agent Brennan Colton had always loved New York City's theater district. The Midtown Manhattan neighborhood between 40th and 54th Streets and 6th and 8th Avenues had always represented the best times and great artistic expression. Just weeks ago, he'd been there with friends to see the musical *& Juliet*. Dinner had followed, the group heading to Nobu Downtown for sashimi and his favorite Wagyu beef served with their warm mushroom salad.

Now, he and patrolmen from the 130th Precinct were walking from theater to theater searching for the next potential victim of a high-profile serial killer. Weeks ago, a man named Mark Welden had been found shot to death in the area of Central Park known as the Ramble. There had been a typed note stuffed in his pocket. That note had announced the murderer's intent to kill in the name of serial killer Maeve O'Leary, a woman known as the Black Widow. O'Leary had recently been captured and charged with killing multiple husbands for financial gain. The murderer declared the objective to kill persons whose initials literally spelled out Maeve's name.

Soon after, a second body was found on the observation deck of the Empire State Building. His name was Andrew Capowski, and he also had a note in his pocket. Edward Pendleton had been murdered at the Met shortly after. With his last note, the killer had teased that he was jumping to the letter L to confuse them. It made no sense, but it was all they had to work with.

FBI profilers had determined the killer was male, deeply troubled and obsessed with a woman he couldn't have. His victims had all been blond, blue-eyed and in their thirties, another detail pointing them toward the killer. Because of the significant sites where the bodies had been found, the media had dubbed him the Landmark Killer.

The last note had been sent to Brennan's cousin Sinead Colton just days earlier. Sinead was also an agent with the FBI, and that note had pointed them toward Broadway as being the sight of the next murder. Brennan had been singularly focused on the forty Broadway theaters that were located on those streets that intersected Broadway in the Times Square area.

They'd been searching for employees whose names began with the letter L and fit the physical profile of the previous victims.

Finding the Landmark Killer had become personal, and Brennan was willing to dedicate all his energy to searching out the murderer who'd also added harassing and provoking Colton family members to his list of crimes.

An officer, whose name Brennan had forgotten, suddenly tapped him on the shoulder. He jumped, the touch unexpected, as he'd fallen into deep thought.

"Sorry, Agent Colton, but we just got a call. There's been a murder near here. The sergeant thought you might want to follow us to the crime scene."

"Do they think it's our guy?"

The officer shook his head. "Not sure, sir."

Brennan nodded. He took a deep breath, and as the officer turned an about-face, heading in the opposite direction, he followed after him.

Tears streamed down Stella's face. Sirens sounded in the distance, their harsh ring drawing closer and closer. The sirens were soon followed by the heavy patter of footsteps rushing in her direction.

"Put your hands up," someone shouted.

"Move away from the body," someone else hollered.

It was only when she heard the familiar click of guns being chambered that she turned to look over her shoulder. At least a dozen of New York's finest were pointing their weapons in her direction. She felt herself bristle, a flood of grief and fear washing over her.

"I didn't do anything," she shouted back. "He needs an ambulance. Please! Someone help him!"

"Move away from the body and put your hands up!" an officer shouted at her a second time.

Stella gently eased Rockwell's head back to the ground. She pushed herself up and onto her feet. As she took a step back, slowly raising her hands up and over her head, Rockwell gasped. She hesitated, wanting to move back to him, and then he uttered her name, the heavy rasp of his voice vibrating through the air.

"Stella…I'm s…s…s… Oh, Stella…"

Her name was a loud whisper blowing past his thin lips. Then he closed his eyes and blew out his last breath.

Stella was suddenly aware of the many guns pointed in her direction. The police were screaming instructions, and fear hit her like a tidal wave. She was a black woman, alone with the dead body of her ex-boyfriend. His blood stained the front of her blue-and-white striped blouse and covered her hands. Things looked differently from how they actually were, and she knew enough to trust that it would only take one nervous cop with a shaky finger on the trigger of his weapon to change the entire trajectory of all their lives.

"I'm not resisting," she cried out, her arms pushed skyward, her hands open and fingers spread. "I didn't do anything. I found him like this. I called for help," she shouted.

An officer eased behind her. He reached for her right arm and pulled it behind her back. He reached for the other, and then secured her wrists with handcuffs. A second uniformed patrolman grabbed her roughly, pushing her far from the body as EMS personnel hurried to Rockwell's side. The cop manhandling her pushed her to the ground, instructing her to take a seat. Someone else started firing questions at her, wanting to know what she knew. The moment was surreal, and Stella felt like she was lost in another dimension, her world suddenly turned on its head and spinning out of control.

"You have the right to remain silent. Anything you say can and will be used against you in a court of law. You have the right to an attorney. If you cannot afford an attorney, one will be appointed for you."

Stella suddenly balked as an officer began to Mirandize her. "Why am I being arrested? I didn't do anything. I found him like that! I'm a reporter with the *New York Wire*!"

Brennan took in his surroundings as he turned into the alley and moved closer to the crime scene. A forensics team and numerous detectives were already surveilling the area, and he turned to stare in Stella's direction as one of the detectives pointed her out as a potential suspect.

Brennan recognized Stella Maxwell from the professional photograph that always accompanied her byline at the newspaper she worked for. That photo didn't do her justice, because the young woman was breathtaking, in spite of her frazzled expression and the blood splatter on her clothes. He felt something pitch hard in his midsection as he stared, and a loud gasp blew past his thin lips. He ignored the fact that Stella Maxwell had been trying to reach him for weeks now, wanting a comment or interview about his progress with finding the Landmark Killer. He had sent her calls to voice mail and her emails to his trash bin. He had neither needed nor wanted any media attention on the serial killer who was proving to be so elusive.

Now, sitting there, she looked dazed, her teary expression pulling at his heartstrings. He found himself wanting to pull her close, to ease his arms around her torso and comfort her. The rush of emotion was unsettling and totally out of his character. Most especially since he had no idea how she was connected to the dead man now lying under a green tarp.

Stella suddenly called his name, screaming for his attention. "Agent Brennan Colton? Excuse me! Agent Colton, it's me, Stella Maxwell! Stella Maxwell with the *New York Wire*! We've been playing phone tag!"

Brennan took a deep breath as he turned in her direction. He sauntered slowly to where she was sitting. Her expression lifted, an air of anticipation washing over her face. There was something like hope that misted her large brown eyes. Something that punched him hard in the gut and took his breath away.

"Agent Colton, would you tell them who I am,

please," Stella pleaded, those damn eyes of hers imploring him to step in and save her.

Brennan took a deep breath. He exhaled slowly, staring at her intently. "I'm sorry, Ms. Maxwell. I'm sure things will get sorted out down at the station." He turned abruptly, moving toward the detectives who were evaluating the case that had landed in their laps. As he walked away, he found himself feeling like a complete schmuck and not the decent guy his parents had raised.

Minutes later, Stella was settled in the back seat of a patrol car. The muscles in her face had tightened, and she looked as if she might explode. She glared in his direction, and he was suddenly unsettled. His instincts told him she had nothing to do with the murder, but he had no jurisdiction over this investigation. He needed to take a step back while the NYPD did their job. He couldn't afford to make waves with the department. Not as long as he needed their help to find the killer he was after.

Chapter 2

Daggers of ice shot from Stella's eyes as the patrol car pulled out of the alleyway and into midday traffic. Brennan Colton was staring as they took her away, and if she could have told him exactly what she thought about him, it would not have been pretty.

The elusive federal agent had been dodging her efforts to reach him for over a month. She had done everything short of showing up at his front door wearing a clown suit and pretending to be a singing telegram to get his attention. And all she wanted were answers to a few questions that could potentially lead to an award-winning article. Him eluding her was one thing, but for the man to blatantly disregard her cries for help when he could have easily vouched for her was another.

She sat back in the patrol car, fighting not to cry. A tidal wave of emotion was consuming her. It was an imbalance of feelings that had left her completely offsides. She was frightened and sad and angry, and she wasn't sure where to put it all. Someone had killed Rockwell Henley, and although the two had no longer been in a relationship, she had still cared about the man. Even worse, there were those who now assumed because she'd been there, then she must have done it. Such was so far south from the truth that she couldn't imagine anyone thinking she could be guilty.

She and Rockwell had dated for over a year. They'd been good together, until they hadn't been. Rockwell had come from a prominent New York family. His father had been a top political analyst before retiring, and his mother was a world-renowned visual artist. The couple traveled in elite circles, and they'd had grand plans for their only son. His parents had never really liked her, believing that Rockwell could do better, considering their position in high society. They hadn't been shy about showing their disdain for her, tolerating her presence in their son's life because he'd given them no choice.

Rockwell had attended all the right schools. Phillips Exeter Academy for high school, Columbia University for his undergraduate studies and Harvard Law School for his juris doctorate. He'd built a thriving legal firm and had been a rising political star. When he'd announced his candidacy for Governor, Stella had stood dutifully by his side, despite his mother's wish for her to find a hole and fall into it.

Things went left after that. One too many missed fundraisers, and Rockwell had suddenly felt she was too obsessed with her own job to be the woman he needed by his side. Stella hadn't been willing to play the role of a dutiful political wife and partner. Rockwell's eventual quest for the White House was supposed to take priority over her dreams of winning a Pulitzer Prize.

Sadly, letting the relationship go and saying goodbye to Rockwell hadn't been as hard as she'd expected. The moment had been heartbreaking, but then she'd been over it just as quickly as it had taken him to write the text message calling an end to their relationship.

There had been no animosity between them. He'd gone his way and she'd gone hers. Although she hadn't anticipated running into him, since he ran in circles that didn't necessarily include her, she knew they could be cordial with each other if they ever did. They'd made good memories during their time together, and she had truly wished him well. Now her heart hurt for the loss, never imagining when she woke that morning that she would have to mourn his passing.

Stella looked up to find one of the officers staring at her. She stared back, snapping in his direction. "What?" she questioned, her eyes wide and seeping with rage.

The man shrugged but didn't bother to respond. He shot his partner a look, the two men cackling as if she'd said something funny. The driver's gaze shifted to his side mirrors, and then he refocused his attention back to the road and the steady flow of traffic.

Stella turned to stare out the window. She couldn't believe this was happening to her. How could anyone believe that she, Stella Maxwell, was capable of killing anyone? She was always kind and gracious to people. Rarely did she not get along with anyone. Stella made friends with everyone she met. Singularly focused on her career, Stella had worked too hard to get to where she was in the industry to just throw it all away over a relationship that had soured. Someone was setting her up. Someone wanted it to look like she had murdered Rockwell. Someone who knew about the two of them. Someone determined to put Stella through hell.

Although she had bumped heads with people on multiple occasions to get a story, she couldn't begin to fathom who would go to such extremes to do this to her. Who had she pissed off, and why were they seeking retribution?

The patrol car pulled into the side parking garage of the 130th precinct. They were in Midtown Manhattan, on Forty-Second Street, near Lexington Avenue and the Grand Central Station. The entrance led them to an underground space where prisoners were routinely filtered into and out of the building, either headed to court or inside to booking.

The cop who'd been staring at her opened the rear door and gestured for her to get out. He was a slim man, his blue uniform pristine. His dark military haircut framed a round face riddled with acne scars. His cheeks were chipmunk round, as if they were stuffed with acorns. His head was almost bulbous, in comparison to his body frame, seeming too large for his neck, and his dark eyes were a degree from being ice cold.

"I want to speak with your superior," Stella quipped as he grabbed her arm and escorted her toward a large metal door. "And I need to make a telephone call."

The man laughed again, tossing a look around the room. "You'll get your chance," he said finally.

Inside, she was pushed into a chair and told to wait her turn. The room was overcrowded and loud. The dank smell of unwashed bodies saturated her nostrils. For a brief moment, she thought she might vomit, and then she didn't. She muttered under her breath, "Why is this happening? I didn't do anything!"

The woman beside her laughed. "Honey, we are all innocent. I didn't do anything either." She paused. "Except shoot that bitch for messing with my Harry. No one messes with my Harry. Not on my watch."

"You shot her? Dead?"

"No! In the foot!" The woman laughed, her brunette curls shaking like jelly rolls atop her head. "It was just a flesh wound. I don't know why they're making such a big deal out of it."

"Maybe because you shot her," Stella said sarcastically.

The woman bristled. "Aren't you all high and mighty? I heard them whispering about you offing your boyfriend."

"I didn't *off* my boyfriend!"

"Well, since we're both headed to Rikers, I imagine whatever you did is just as bad as me shooting Harry's whore in the foot."

Stella's eyes widened. "Rikers? I'm not going to Rikers!" she said, shaking her head vehemently.

The woman laughed at her again. "We all go to Rikers," she said nonchalantly.

Stella jumped from her seat, moving toward the counter at the front of the room.

An officer held out his arm, his other hand resting on the weapon at his waistband. "Sit down!" he shouted.

Tears pressed hot against Stella's lids. "I really need to make a call," she said. "There's been a horrible mistake."

"I said…sit…down!" The man snapped at her, taking a step in her direction.

"It's okay," a voice said, the firm tone vibrating through the room. "Escort Miss Maxwell to an interrogation room, please."

Stella turned to see a woman in the doorway staring at her, her vibrant green eyes serious and intense. She was petite in stature but clearly had a large presence at the station. Her dark hair was cut in a cute pixie style, and she wore a white blouse, khaki slacks and a shiny silver badge clipped to her belt. She gestured with her head and the other officer nodded.

"Yes, ma'am, Detective Colton."

Stella's brow raised. "Colton? Are you…" she started to say, curiosity perched on the tip of her tongue.

The officer grabbed her arm, stalling the question

she was trying to formulate and ask. He pulled Stella forward and led her away in the opposite direction.

They were being too nice to her, Stella thought, feeling like the last hour was only the calm before the storm to come. A uniformed officer had allowed her to use the restroom and had brought her a glass of ice water. They'd offered her a cup of coffee and a sandwich and had finally removed the handcuffs that had begun to cut off her circulation. She rubbed at her wrists, her gaze moving to the large two-way mirror that made up one wall.

Stella wondered who was on the other side and why they were waiting to speak with her. She was past ready to be done with all of this so she could head home. Home was calling her. Loudly. Home was where she found peace and tranquility and could shut the world away without feeling guilty. She needed to be home if she was going to survive the day without really killing someone. She blew a heavy sigh and pushed herself from the table, beginning to pace the room.

Another hour passed before the door swung open and two plainclothes detectives entered the room. One reminded her of Pat Sajak from the game show *Wheel of Fortune*. The other was a dead ringer for Peter Griffin from the adult cartoon *Family Guy*. He had the same exaggerated chin, a bulging neckline, a beer belly and chocolate brown hair cut into a low beanie. Stella eyed them both with reservation, her gaze sweeping from one to the other.

"Ms. Maxwell, please, have a seat," the Peter Griffin doppelganger said. He nodded his head toward the chair she'd occupied minutes before. "Sorry to keep you waiting. My name is Detective Voorhies, and this is Detective Palmer."

The man named Palmer tossed her a slight wave of his hand. "We were hoping you'd be ready to make a statement so we can get you out of here."

Stella's gaze narrowed. "I was ready to get out of here hours ago, which is why I made a statement before I was dragged in here." Her voice rose an octave. "I have nothing to hide, Detective! I've shown you my phone and the text message that came in saying a man was being murdered. You can trace the telephone call that came into my office right before that. I've told you everything I know! At this point, all I can do is repeat myself. Again."

Detective Palmer forced a smile on his face. "Although we can appreciate your enthusiasm, we hope that you understand that under the circumstances, we do have protocols we need to follow." He scribbled something across the top of a sheet of paper. "Can you confirm your address for me?"

There was a moment's hesitation as Stella considered his request. Stella knew the routine. She knew they'd process her background information first, insuring she was who she said she was. She knew they would need to confirm her pedigree before they processed her arrest. She was also fully aware that anything she said, either orally or in writing, would go straight to the prosecutor, and its admissibility could derail any defense if they were ever to go to trial. She had no doubt that promising her she could go home was a ploy to get a confession out of her.

"Do you have a suspect?" she asked instead. "Any idea who might have done this?"

Detective Voorhies leaned back in his chair, crossing his arms over his belly. "We're interested in knowing what you think. I understand from Mr. Henley's mother that you and he recently ended a relationship. She says he broke up with you. I imagine that might have made you mad."

"You imagine wrong," she said, a hint of snark in her tone. "We had both agreed that it was for the best."

"You sure about that? I understand there were some heated text messages between you and the victim."

Stella felt her cheeks redden. Knowing that the last conversation between her and Rockwell was now being leveraged against her was embarrassing. And infuriating. She had no doubt that his mother couldn't wait to tell them it had all been her fault.

Palmer chimed in with his two cents. "Look at it from our perspective, Ms. Maxwell. You had motive, opportunity and means. You were the only one in that alley with the victim, and your fingerprints were on the murder weapon. So let's not play this game. Just tell us what happened. Was it a moment of passion? Were you two arguing? We'd understand if things went left when you were just trying to have a conversation with Mr. Henley."

Stella felt her entire body tense. She'd flinched, and she was certain it hadn't gone unnoticed. She shook her head vehemently. "There's no way my fingerprints are on the murder weapon," she snapped. "I never touched that knife!"

"Really, Ms. Maxwell. Let's not do this. You're going to have to tell us something. We will find out the truth."

Stella met the smug look the man was giving her. "I'd like an attorney," she said, sitting back in her own chair.

Detective Voorhies shot his partner a look. "That's fine, but all we want to know is—"

Stella pushed her palm toward his face, interrupting him. "I don't give a rat's ass what you want to know. I want my attorney," she said harshly.

Voorhies suddenly looked like a fish out of water, his mouth opening and then closing as if he needed to suck in air. He stood and Palmer followed his lead. "That's fine. We were willing to work with you, but if you—"

"Why are you still talking?" Stella snapped. "I said I want my attorney. That's the end of our conversation, or are you purposely planning to violate my rights?"

The man's expression was somber as the duo turned from her and made their way out the door. As it closed behind them, Stella turned her attention toward the two-way mirror, staring as if she could see who was standing on the other side. She suddenly grabbed the Styrofoam cup filled with water and flung it at the glass with every ounce of energy she could muster.

"Is that your best?" she raged. "You're going to need to do better than those two bozos!"

She paused, seeming to wait for something, or someone, to respond. Finally, she shook her head. "I didn't kill him," she said, her voice dropping to a loud whisper. "I didn't do it!"

Chapter 3

Rory Colton tossed her cousin Brennan a look. "Don't you dare laugh," she quipped. "If you laugh, I will hurt you."

Brennan held up his hands as if he were surrendering. "Did they really think they could break her?" he asked.

His cousin shook her head. "Who the hell knows what those two were thinking?"

The duo stood on the other side of that two-way mirror eyeing Stella. After her outburst, she'd paced the room for a good ten minutes before dropping back into the chair. Her arms were folded over her chest defiantly. Her expression was cold.

"What's your gut tell you?" Rory asked, turning to study her cousin's expression.

"She didn't do it."

"Her fingerprints are on the weapon. How do you explain that?"

Brennan shrugged. "I can't. But then I'm not investigating this case. Not officially."

"Like I need one more thing on my plate," Rory muttered.

"I know the feeling," Brennan said. He thought about his own case and his need to get the Landmark Killer off the streets. The muscles in his face pulled into a deep frown.

Rory gave him a nod. "Well, you know we'll do everything we can here to help you out."

"I appreciate that. I really do."

There was suddenly a knock on the door. The two looked up as the entrance opened and one of the station's secretaries gestured for Rory's attention.

"I'll be back," Rory said, excusing herself from the room. "Try to stay out of trouble while I'm gone, please."

Brennan chuckled softly. "When do I ever get in trouble?"

As the door closed after Rory, Brennan turned his attention back to the woman in the other room. The smile that had been on his face fell into another sober frown. She was still sitting, staring out into space as she waited patiently for the NYPD to decide what they planned to do with her. If he could have carried the weight she was shouldering, he would have done so gladly. He would have done almost anything to put a smile on her face. He suddenly felt as if he'd fallen down and hit his head, every ounce of sanity gone from him.

Even in her sadness, she was still stunning. She drew her fingers through the length of her hair, the dark black strands falling past her shoulders. Her crystal complexion was a warm pecan, and she wore the barest hint of makeup. Her features were sculpted, complementing dark brown eyes, full pouty lips and a near-perfect button nose.

She stood and began to pace the room one more time. She was tall and willowy, definitely more leg than torso, he thought. She moved with the grace of a professional ballet dancer, and there was something almost ethereal about her presence. Standing there watching her, he was slightly mesmerized, unable to shift his gaze from her. But his thoughts were elsewhere, unable to focus on anything other than what he'd been sent there to investigate.

Although he wasn't privy to all the details about the murder Stella had been accused of, Brennan knew enough to say the death of political candidate Rockwell Henley was in no way connected to those of the Landmark Killer. He didn't fit the profile, and that killer had been meticulous about staying on script. This was something else, and now it too was consuming his thoughts.

Rory returned minutes later. "We need to cut her loose," she said, gesturing for him to follow after her.

"What's up?" Brennan questioned.

"We have an eyewitness to the murder. And video tape that clears Ms. Maxwell of any wrongdoing."

"I may need to see that video tape," Brennan said as he headed toward the door behind her.

Rory shook her head. "How did I know you were going to say that?" she said.

Stella was ready to blow a gasket when the door swung open and the Colton woman from earlier moved inside. She carried a laptop computer in her hands. Brennan Colton followed on her heels. His sheepish expression only infuriated Stella even more. She tossed up her hands in frustration.

"Either get me my attorney and charge me, or I'm leaving!" Stella snapped.

There was a moment's pause as all three took a deep breath, blowing stale air out slowly.

"Ms. Maxwell, I'm Detective Rory Colton. If we can please talk for a moment."

"No! I'm done talking. I'm leaving!"

"I understand your frustration. I also have no doubt that you know we can hold you for seventy-two hours."

"Seventy-two hours! For what? I didn't do anything!"

"And we now know that. I'm hoping that you might be able to help us identify who did kill Mr. Henley." The woman's voice was calming, her tone even.

Rory's green eyes stared at her, and Stella found her gaze like an easy balm. She took another breath, then moved back to the table and sat down. Rory moved to the seat opposite her. Brennan was still standing, leaning back against the wall, his hands pushed deep into his pockets.

"We have video of the murder. I'm hoping you might recognize the killer," Rory said.

"Video?"

Rory nodded. "A tourist caught the murder on film. He was doing a panoramic video of the street and wasn't paying attention to everything he was filming. He didn't realize what he had until he went back to his hotel room and played the footage. When he saw he'd captured the murder, he brought it right to the police department."

Stella leaned forward as Rory opened the laptop and pushed the Play button on the device. The video on the screen was clear but devoid of sound. Rockwell stood in the alley wringing his hands together. Clearly, he was waiting for someone, and Stella couldn't help but wonder who or what had made him come. Why had Rockwell been there?

She watched as a figure in a black hoodie and mask, hands in the front pouch, moved to Rockwell's side. There was a heated exchange between the two, the duo arguing like they were familiar with each other, and then gloved hands pulled a large butcher knife from inside that hoodie.

The assault was unexpected, Rockwell caught off guard with the first jab. He was stabbed repeatedly until he fell to the ground. The killer hovered above him just briefly, then pushed their hands back into the pockets of that hoodie and hurried toward the street, disappearing into the crowd. Just moments later, Stella is seen arriving, finding Rockwell injured.

Tears sprang to her eyes as the video replayed her

trepidation as she approached the body, the shock of recognition, the inhalation of her breath catching in her throat, her screams for help and the tears that had rained over her cheeks. It also captured the guns pointed toward her, more officers surrounding her than she had initially realized.

She sat back, her head shaking slowly from side to side. It was enough to have her crying again, but she pushed the emotion down, refusing to let one tear spill. Most especially with Brennan Colton in the room.

Rory pushed the pause button on the laptop to stop the video. "Was there anything familiar about our suspect? Anything you recognize that might help us identify them?"

"No," Stella said, her voice a loud whisper. "Sorry, but no." She inhaled, a deep breath filling her lungs. "I think they knew each other though. The way they were arguing. Rockwell knew his killer."

Rory nodded. "We were thinking the same thing."

"The other detective said my fingerprints were on the murder weapon. Was that true?" Stella questioned.

"Yes, it is. Do you have any idea how that could be?"

She shook her head. "No. But someone's gone to a lot of trouble to frame me."

"Any idea who has that kind of grudge against you?"

Stella's gaze dropped to the table as she fell into thought. Over the years she'd probably made more enemies than friends if she was honest with herself. In her line of work, it had always been about the story, no matter the casualties left from her pushing for facts and truth. But she couldn't think of anyone who would have gone to such lengths to get even with her for doing her job and doing her job well.

She shook her head again. "No," she answered. "I don't have a clue who could have done this." She didn't bother to say that not knowing had her unsettled. Her eyes shifted toward Brennan, who was eyeing her intently.

She found his stare unsettling, his baby blue eyes igniting a wave of heat through her body that was neither expected nor wanted. He was lean and wiry, the suit he wore meticulously cut to his slim frame. He pushed the short length of his pale, blond hair off his forehead, and she gasped at the sheer beauty of him. Why did he have to be so good-looking, she pondered?

Her gaze narrowed substantially, her ire rising once again. She folded her hands over her chest. "Why didn't you vouch for me?" she suddenly asked, her gaze locked on his face. "Why would you let them drag me in here like I was a common criminal? And they put me in a jail cell!" she snarled, her voice rising.

Brennan took a step forward. "Sorry about that. But I had to follow protocols, and this isn't my jurisdiction. Besides, I knew *who* you were, but we really don't *know* each other."

"Maybe if you had answered just one of my calls over the last few weeks, we would have known each other. I think you're just a jerk. You could have helped me," Stella snapped.

"I've been called worse," Brennan said.

"He has," Rory interjected. "But in his defense, I don't think my cousin was trying to intentionally dismiss you. He's not that kind of guy."

Stella looked from one to the other. "He's still an ass!" she quipped, not an ounce of forgiveness in sight.

"I'll take that," Brennan said, a wide smile pulling across his face. "Now let me take you to dinner to apologize and make up for my mishap."

"You have fallen and cracked your skull if you think for one second I want to have anything to do with you now," Stella responded. She turned her attention back to Rory. "Am I free to leave?"

The detective nodded. "You are. I may have more questions for you later."

"Yeah, yeah!" Stella said snidely as she moved back onto her feet and headed toward the door. "I'll try not to leave town!"

"Can I give you a ride home?" Brennan asked. He took a step toward her.

"You can stay the hell away from me," Stella retorted. "I would rather crawl across Manhattan on my hands and knees before I ever ask you for anything again."

"Even a one-on-one interview?"

Stella's glare could have frozen hell. She heard Brennan chuckle softly as she swept past him, not bothering to respond to his comment.

* * *

"I think that went well," Brennan said as he stole a quick glance toward his cousin.

Rory laughed. "If you were trying to crash and burn, I think it went very well."

"How long do you think she'll stay mad at me?"

"You might not ever recover from this. Sorry."

"Why are you apologizing?"

"Because I think you might actually like the woman. And given a chance, she might have actually liked you back."

He shrugged his shoulders, not certain he would agree with her. He had never known any woman who had ever gotten past being that angry with him. That kind of anger usually ended his relationships, so any effort to potentially start one didn't stand much of a chance, he mused.

Stella had made a pit stop at the women's restroom before returning to the front desk to retrieve her personal possessions. Brennan debated whether or not to wait for her and try again. He genuinely felt bad about everything that had happened, but his feelings were bruised by her flagrant rejection. He figured there was no point in letting her scorch what was left of his emotions.

From where he stood, he could see her standing off in a corner on her cell phone. He imagined she needed to let family and friends know that she was well. He wondered if there was a new boyfriend or lover in her life, someone who would hear the details of her day and be there to console her feelings. The thought suddenly had him feeling slightly anxious, something like jealousy coursing through his bloodstream. He shook away the sensation and watched as she finally ended her call and headed toward the building's front entrance.

Stella was still angry enough to kick rocks. She'd missed her meeting at the middle school and a meeting with the marketing department. One of her sources had left six messages for her and now wasn't answering her return call. The senior editor had left a message also, spewing words that shouldn't be spoken in proper company. And Rockwell's murder had made the breaking news, his parents vowing to ensure the killer would be found and justice would be served. Although they hadn't mentioned her name, a quick profile image of her in the police car had made the news loop, calling her a person of interest who was being questioned. Anyone who knew her wouldn't have much of a problem recognizing her, and now she was even angrier.

As she moved toward the front door of the police station, she thought about calling for a ride but reasoned she shouldn't have too much trouble waving down a yellow cab. Before stepping out into the afternoon air, Stella turned, looking around the room in search of Brennan. She hoped to see him one last time, to glare in his direction so that he was reminded once more that she wasn't happy with him. To catch one more glimpse of the man whose dazzling smile and boy-next-door good looks had taken her breath away. To remind herself, and him, that he was a complete and total idiot and that had he played his cards right, things could have been so good between them. Not that she really believed that, but she was feeling petty, which necessitated a unique level of bitchiness that Stella had mastered by the time she'd been twelve years old.

Her gaze skated around the space, and then there he was. His back was to her as he moved through a door on the other side of the room. As he disappeared from her sight, Stella turned and stormed out the entrance.

Chapter 4

Brennan was still thinking about his case, the other murder and Stella Maxwell. It had been close to an hour since the beautiful woman had been released. He had hoped to see her before she'd made her exit, but Rory had commanded his attention, wanting an update on the Landmark Killer case and the FBI's thoughts on the killer's next steps. Despite wanting to make sure Stella was well, he still had a job to do, and business came before all else.

Exiting the police station to head to his own office, he was surprised to find Stella standing on the sidewalk, her cell phone still attached to her ear. She was deep in conversation with someone, and frustration still furrowed her brow. At the sight of her, a wave of excitement began to build in his midsection, and he felt his face pull into a wide grin.

As he began to inch his way closer, he realized she too had shifted into business mode, the conversation sounding as if it were centered around an article she'd either written or needed to write. She wasn't happy and had no problems letting the other party know how she felt.

There was something about Stella that Brennan found engaging. She spoke her mind, not bothering to hold her tongue under any circumstances. He had no doubt that she could hold a grudge for longer than most, and did just to be contrary. While he'd hoped she'd had some time to cool off, it was likely she hadn't and would still be angry with him. He braced himself, taking a deep inhale of breath as he took another step closer.

He noticed the white paneled delivery van before she did. It was the third time the vehicle had circled the block. He'd dismissed it the first two times, thinking the driver was likely having difficulty finding a parking space to make a delivery. New York traffic and the ability to park had its own reputation and wasn't talked about kindly. This time the van slowed down substantially as it eased into a no-parking zone near where Stella was standing. Intuition told Brennan something was amiss, but he wasn't certain what suddenly had his antennae on edge.

A uniformed police officer standing on the steps near him gestured toward the driver, yelling for him to move. There was a moment of hesitation, and with the tinted windows, Brennan wasn't able to see the driver's face or expression. He imagined the man or woman wasn't happy about being shooed away.

The van eased back into traffic and turned at the corner. Stella had tossed the officer and then the van a look. When she turned back, she noticed Brennan standing there staring at her. She turned toward him, still talking on her phone as people pushed dismissively past her. The look she gave him still held a lot of hostility, he thought. Brennan tossed up his hand in an awkward wave. Stella's gaze narrowed, and then she turned her back to him, stepping closer to the street as she reached out a hand to wave down a taxi. Clearly, Brennan thought, Stella was still angry with him.

Thinking it might be better if he gave her some more time, Brennan turned to head in the opposite direction. As he spun an about-face, he saw the van from earlier round the corner once again. This time the driver didn't slow down. Instead, they moved swiftly toward the empty space beside Stella, coming to an abrupt stop in front of her. The side door slid open and two masked men wearing all black jumped from inside. Just seconds later, Stella's screams were piercing through the late afternoon air.

Stella was still seething, and seeing Brennan standing at the door of the police station watching her had further fueled her rage. Contending with the fallout from her arrest had started with those missed calls and looked like it was about to end with her being suspended from her job. She and her boss had been going back and forth over the phone, him insisting that she take a personal leave of absence until things blew over. She didn't need, or want, a compulsory vacation. She needed to work, and the senior editor wasn't interested in hearing that. To add insult to injury, he'd had the audacity to ask her for an exclusive statement about her arrest and the murder of Rockwell Henley. She'd told him in no uncertain terms what he could do with that request, albeit politely worded and in a calm tone. Heaven forbid she risk being labeled an angry black woman, no matter how angry she might have been about her situation.

Stepping off the curb, she waved at a passing taxi, hopeful that it would stop and pick her up. She knew she was just a few short blocks from a tunnel entrance, and she could have taken the subway back to Harlem, but she didn't have the patience. Not right then.

After the third taxi passed her by, she was starting to feel broken, her rage having morphed into something she couldn't describe. It had taken on a life of its own, and she struggled not to burst into an ugly cry. She tossed a quick glance over her shoulder to see if Brennan was still watching her. She wished him away, and as if her prayers were being answered, he turned an about-face and headed in the opposite direction. She turned back to the task at hand but was surprised when a large white van suddenly pulled up before her, blocking her view.

As she heaved a deep sigh to quell her emotions,

the van's door slid open, and two men jumped from inside. At first, Stella didn't think anything of the masks they wore, their all-black attire giving them the appearance of cat burglars. It was New York, and people were known to wear a variety of attire to suit their moods. For all she knew, they could have been making a fashion statement. Masks had become a daily staple for many, the entire city once guarding themselves from the ravages of the COVID pandemic. Even she wore a mask when riding the subway.

As she moved to step aside, one man grabbed her arm roughly. The other began to push her toward the vehicle's door, and Stella began to scream like her life depended on it.

Everything was a blur. Stella's handbag and phone fell to the ground as she kicked and screamed. She was a banshee on high heels as she drew as much attention to her attackers as she could. It was a take-no-prisoner's moment as Stella clawed and punched and tried to inflict as much harm as she could muster.

Rushing to her side, Brennan threw his own punch, sending one of the men backward against the vehicle. He grabbed Stella around the waist and swung her away from the other, putting himself between her and them. As he reached for the gun holstered at his waist, both men jumped back into the van. It careened into traffic and headed swiftly down the street. As quickly as they had appeared, they had disappeared. The moment was surreal, no more than three minutes passing from start to finish. Stella was suddenly surrounded by police officers for the second time that day.

"Anyone get the license plate?" Brennan shouted. He slowly eased his gun back into its holster.

"Running it now," someone shouted back. "And we have a car on its tail."

Brennan turned his attention back to Stella. He gripped her gently by the shoulders. "Are you okay? Did you get hurt?" he questioned.

She shook her head. "I'm fine," she snapped. She shook herself from his grip, unsettled by his touch. "Really, I'm okay."

"Did you recognize anyone?"

She shook her head, those tears finally falling past the length of her dark lashes. "No!" she said, her voice a loud whisper. "Why would someone—" she started to say.

Rory interrupted, rushing to their side. "What happened?" she questioned. "One of my officers said there was a kidnapping in progress?"

Brennan nodded. "Stella was attacked. Two men tried to pull her into their van," he said.

Rory's eyes widened. "In broad daylight?"

"Criminals have no qualms about committing their crimes when it's inconvenient for the rest of us," Brennan said snidely.

Rory rolled her eyes at her cousin. She turned her attention to Stella. "We should get you inside," she said. "We can review the surveillance tape. Maybe you'll recognize something."

Stella had knelt down to pick up her personal possessions from the ground. She dropped her phone, a tube of lip gloss and her change purse back inside.

She shook her head vehemently once she was standing upright, her purse strap back on her shoulder. "No. I'm going home. I am done with you people."

"It might not be safe—" Rory began to say.

"Obviously, I'm not safe standing here in front of the damn police station," Stella snapped. "I'm going home!"

Rory looked to her cousin for assistance. Brennan shrugged his shoulders.

"I'll take you," Brennan said, shifting his gaze back to Stella.

She started to argue, but he interrupted her. "I insist."

Before Stella could give him a hard time, he cupped his hand beneath her elbow and gently guided her in the direction of his car. He called out to his cousin over his shoulder. "I've got her. Give her some time. I'll get the answers you need."

Stella shot him a look, her head shaking from side to side at his arrogance. He didn't have a clue what he did or did not have. And despite what he might have been hoping, what he did not have was unfettered access to her.

Brennan took East Drive to Madison Avenue, following it north out of lower Manhattan into West Harlem. Stella didn't bother to give him directions, and Brennan didn't ask the way to her home. Under different circumstances, she might have been disturbed by him knowing where she lived. These circumstances were unique, and it barely moved the dial on her personal radar.

She reasoned he'd probably researched her as much as she'd researched him. Her being in police custody had also given him access to her personal information had he been interested in knowing it. Clearly, he'd been interested, as he headed in the right direction.

She stared out the passenger window, not bothering to acknowledge him. He hadn't said much himself, not bothering with casual small talk. He seemed to understand that she needed time and space, and he was still far from being her favorite person. When he took the turn onto West 136th Street, she shifted in her seat, taking a deep inhale of air into her lungs.

"You can drop me off—"

"I'm not leaving you. Not until we can figure out who tried to set you up for killing your boyfriend. And who just tried to grab you."

"My ex-boyfriend," Stella said, as if the correction to disassociate herself from Rockwell would somehow make things better. "And I have been racking my head trying to figure out who could be doing all this. I mean…why would someone try to grab me in front of the police station, of all places? How did they know I'd be there? I mean…is it possible it had nothing to do with Rock's murder, and I just happened to be in the wrong place at the wrong time?"

"Anything's possible, but I don't believe in coincidences," Brennan said.

Stella took another breath. "Neither do I," she said. "I was just hoping something might make sense."

"Well, I suggest we pool our collective resources and work together. Two heads being better than one and all that." He gave her a smile before turning his attention back to the roadway and the traffic that had slowed their progress.

"I don't need your help, and I don't need a baby-sitter."

"Well, I'm not a very good babysitter," he said. "Just ask my family. I've lost a few of them, bumped one's head against a door, and if I remember correctly, picked up the wrong kid from day care trying to help out my boss. It wasn't pretty!"

Stella laughed, amusement painting her expression. She appreciated his attempts at humor, although he clearly wasn't going to win any awards for his comedic efforts.

She suddenly changed the subject. "Why didn't you return my calls?"

Brennan gave her a quick glance. He answered her matter-of-factly. "Because you were a royal pain in my ass. Obviously, if I didn't answer, you should have taken that as a hint I wasn't interested in talking to you. Clearly, I didn't have any answers for you or anything to say for your story."

"You could have said just that. I had only hoped to keep people informed about the investigation so they would know you were actually out there doing something. You would not be the first person to tell me no. I could have accepted your rejection. But you were just out and out rude."

Brennan shrugged. "I don't agree."

Stella shrugged her own shoulders. "I didn't expect that you would, Agent Colton."

Brennan didn't bother to hide his surprise at Stella's Harlem address. Although it had been some time since he was last in that end of the Manhattan borough, it was an area and neighborhood he was familiar with. Brennan had family who'd once lived in the area. It was also not far from the property the former president Bill Clinton had moved his offices. Although it had been some twenty-plus years since he'd moved in, much had been said about the rapid gentrification of an area that had once been predominantly African American. Harlem had been home to thousands of African American families and had been the cultural apex for the community. Businesses were owned and operated by Blacks, and houses were affordable for working class families. As Harlem started seeing gentrification, both businesses and houses became a place where African Americans could no longer afford to live in. Residents who had spent their entire lives in Harlem were forced to move elsewhere. The dynamics of the entire area changed.

Stella's home was in close proximity to parks, public transportation and landmarks like Strivers Row, the Apollo Theater, Columbia University, City University of New York, Barnard College and less than a mile from five major subway stops. It was situated close to the Henry Hudson Parkway so that she could get downtown, uptown or out of town easily. It was prime New York real estate.

Stella led the way to the front door of a beautifully remodeled townhouse in Central Harlem's St. Nicholas Historic District. It was an elegant three-story structure with a professionally landscaped backyard. The classic facade had been impeccably restored, harkening to the days of the Harlem Renaissance.

Spanning three floors, the stunning home welcomed Brennan with an open layout on the parlor floor, exposed brick walls, high ceilings and exquisite hardwood floors. The sun-filled living area spilled over to the dining area and an open chef's kitchen. The eat-in dining space featured plenty of storage room, all new stainless-steel appliances, including a wine cooler and a large open island. Brennan could only begin to imagine what visual delights the other levels held.

He followed on Stella's heels as she led him into the living room and gestured for him to take a seat. His eyes followed after her as she dropped her purse onto an end table and moved to a corner bar, where she pulled two lead-bottomed tumblers from the shelf. She reached for a bottle of bourbon and filled both glasses. She moved back to his side, passed him a glass then dropped down onto the sofa beside him as she rested the bottle on the coffee table.

"This is very nice," Brennan said as he took a sip of the beverage. "If you don't mind my asking, what's the square footage?"

Stella shrugged. "It's just a little over four thousand square feet."

"It's a big house for one person. It's not at all what

I expected. I might need to reconsider my own career choices. The rent here has to be…what…close to four, maybe five thousand per month?"

Stella rolled her eyes skyward. Her impatient look was like an arrow of ice thrown in his direction. "I wouldn't know," she responded, her tone equally as chilly. "I own it and I don't have a mortgage. Anything else you want to know, Agent Colton?"

Brennan swiped at his brow, his cheeks reddening with embarrassment. "Sorry! I didn't mean to get into your personal business."

"Yes, you did!"

Brennan grinned as he nodded his head. "Yes, I did. I was being nosy. But I really didn't mean to be rude about it." A hint of contrition creased his brow.

She shook her head. "Next time just ask me what you want to know. Be direct. Don't beat around the bush. I hate when men do that."

He nodded again, still unsure how to question what was still clearly on his mind. Stella answered as if she could read the thoughts spinning through his head.

"The house was built back in 1910. My great-grandparents were the first family to own it, and they passed it down to my grandfather. I was raised in this house, and I inherited it debt-free from my parents. That's how I can afford to live in a multi-million-dollar home on a journalist's salary," she said sarcastically. "Does that answer your question?"

Brennan's eyes widened. He felt embarrassed that she had read him so well and was saddened about her loss. "Your parents… They've both passed?"

Stella nodded. "My mother when I was twelve, and my father died six years ago."

"I'm so sorry. I know how that feels. I was young when we lost my father too."

"Your mom is still alive?"

Brennan nodded. "She lives in Florida, now. I was lucky to have a big family to lean on. My siblings understood what I was feeling, so we had each other to commiserate with. I hate that you had to endure that kind of hurt alone."

Stella shrugged. "We do what we have to do. How many of you Coltons are there?" she asked, realizing she knew very little of his personal life.

Brennan smiled. "Well, there's my twin brother, Cashel. Cash for short, but when you meet him, call him Cashel. He hates it!"

Stella chuckled. "Not fond of St. Patrick's Rock of Cashel, huh?"

"I'm impressed you know it."

"Don't be. I visited Ireland for my twenty-fifth birthday."

"Even more impressed," Brennan said. "I've never been to Ireland. Or out of the country, for that matter."

"We'll need to work on that. I love to travel. Morocco's next on my bucket list."

Brennan smiled, noting her use of the word *we* in her comment.

She shook her head. "So, is it just you and Cashel?"

"No, there's my brother Patrick, who would technically be the middle kid, and our baby sister Ashlyn. Then of course, if you start counting cousins…" His voice trailed off.

"Wow! That is a large family, especially if you're an only child with no cousins. Are you all close?"

"I wouldn't say that," Brennan quipped. "We have our issues. There's some dysfunction, but I like to think that the love we have for each other makes up for the rest."

Stella pondered the comment, but she didn't respond. She reached for the bourbon bottle and filled her glass a second time. She changed the subject. "I need a shower. Make yourself comfortable," she said, rising from her seat and heading toward the door. "We can talk more when I'm done."

As she reached the bottom of the stairwell, Brennan called her name, meeting her stare evenly as she turned to give him a curious look.

"Yes?"

"I'm really not the jerk you think I am."

Stella hesitated as she considered the comment. She chuckled softly. "That's yet to be determined, Agent Colton."

He smiled. "I look forward to proving it to you."

Chapter 5

Brennan sat with his own thoughts for a few minutes. He could only imagine what Stella was doing up on the floor above, and those things he was thinking had him offsides. For a brief moment he pondered what might happen if he were to venture up those stairs into that shower with her. Heat rippled through his southern quadrant at the perverted thoughts, and he bit down on his bottom lip. And then he considered the pain he knew she would inflict upon his person if he were to even try. They were still establishing boundaries, and although he reasoned it would be nice to know her better, he also sensed that she wasn't interested in being his friend and definitely not his lover. He pondered how he might change her opinion of him, considering her rage had waned substantially since he'd driven her home. Despite his best efforts, another wave of salacious thoughts crossed his mind. Maybe he was a jerk, he mused. Brennan needed to do better, he thought. But he was still very much a man, and she was very much the most desirable woman he'd met in quite some time. But he was getting way ahead of himself, and for the life of him, he couldn't begin to explain why.

Steam billowed through the master bathroom in soft swells. Stella stood beneath a flow of hot water, allowing it to beat gently against her narrow shoulders and over her back. Tears rained from her eyes, falling past the round of her dimpled cheeks. Stella didn't cry often, but the day had left her emotionally depleted, and crying was all she could manage to do. She cried as if she'd lost her best friend, and in some ways, she had. She sobbed as if her cat was gone. If she liked cats. In that moment, there was little that Stella liked or even imagined herself being fond of. All she wanted was to turn back time and get a do-over for the entire day. Maybe even the week, she thought.

Instead, she had to figure out who had murdered Rockwell and why they were trying to pin the offense on her. She had more questions than she had answers. Who had lured Rockwell to that alley, and what reason had they used to bait him there? Had he gone expecting her to make an appearance? Had he been ambushed, hopeful for one thing and surprised by another? Who would brazenly stick a butcher knife in his chest in broad daylight and not expect to get caught? Or was getting caught their objective once they were done toying with her emotions?

She blew a soft sigh as she lifted her face to the spray of water, allowing the droplets to wash away her tears. Her thoughts wandered to the man downstairs in her living room. Brennan was too cute for his own good. And likeable. She found it difficult to stay angry at him, and staying angry would have kept a large enough wall between them that she wouldn't be thinking about his hands trailing down her torso, allowed to play with her girl parts. He left her heated in the most pleasurable way, and Stella knew she had no business thinking of him like that. Nothing could happen between them. Not one damn thing that could leave her vulnerable with a broken heart. But for the life of her, she couldn't get him off her mind. With a shake of her head, Stella reached for the water faucet and turned it to cool.

When Stella bounded back down the stairs and sauntered into the kitchen, Brennan was pulling a baking dish out of her oven. She took a deep inhale of breath, savoring the decadent aroma wafting through the room.

"What's that?" she asked. "It smells really good."

Brennan smiled as he placed the dish on the stove and lay kitchen mitts onto the counter. "It's chicken and rice in a rich cream sauce. One of my many specialties."

"A man who cooks. I'm impressed."

"You will soon discover that I'm a man of many

talents." The grin that spread across his face was canyon wide. "Why don't you set the table," he said, the comment more command than request.

Stella's brow rose ever so slightly as she considered the order. Any man making demands of her in her home would pinch her the wrong way. But Brennan doing it wasn't nearly as disconcerting as she would have expected. She took a deep breath and let the facts of that wash over her. When those thoughts starting heading toward things more decadent, she shook away the reverie she'd fallen into and nodded. She reasoned that she had more important things that needed to be done so that he could go home and get out of her personal space and her head.

Moving to the cupboards, she pulled plates and glasses from inside and then gathered silverware from a drawer near the fridge. Right off the kitchen was a massive wood deck that overlooked her private backyard. It was still hot outside, and Stella thought that they could dine alfresco. She added two place settings on the wrought iron table and then headed back inside to select a bottle of wine from the wine chiller.

"Sauvignon blanc or chardonnay?" she asked, tossing Brennan a quick look.

He hesitated, then shrugged his shoulders. "You choose. I'm good with either."

"Moscato it is, then," Stella said with the softest chuckle.

Brennan laughed. "If that's what we're doing, then I'd prefer a beer," he said.

Minutes later they were seated on the patio. The

sun was still shining, but there was a sweet breeze blowing gently through the warm evening air. The end of the day for both was proving to be far better than how things had started.

Stella took a sip of her wine and rested the glass on the table. "You never did say how you showed up to the crime scene as quickly as you did."

Brennan set his own bottle of beer down. "We were working on the Landmark Killer case down in the theater district. When the call came in, they thought it might be related to that case."

Stella nodded. "Interesting…" she muttered.

"Not really."

"How's that case going?"

Brennan gave her a narrowed gaze. He hesitated for a brief moment. "I'd love to tell you, but I can't risk you sharing the information with your readers."

Stella laughed, her head bobbing up and down. "That's fair. Since our current situation is a little strange, I'm willing to agree to keep anything shared within these walls *off* the record."

"*Off* the record?" Brennan echoed.

Stella held up her right hand before pressing it to her chest. "Cross my heart," she said, a bright smile on her face. She motioned for him to continue. As she did, she crossed the fingers on her other hand and made a grand gesture of pulling her arm behind her back.

Brennan laughed, his head shaking from side to side. "Nope," he said. "I can't with you!"

"Seriously," Stella said. She looked him in the eye, her stare even with his. "I won't do that to you. I'm a woman of my word. If you want to share, then share. I promise it will stay between the two of us, and it won't go on the record."

Brennan took a deep breath. There was something in the look she gave him. He felt a level of trust and understanding that he hadn't expected. He trusted her, and that spoke volumes since he knew so little about her.

He began to speak, seeming to unburden himself from the thoughts running through his head. "We're pretty certain we know *where* he'll hit next. We were hoping to find *who* he might target based on the clues from the previous murders."

"And you're certain the killer is male?" Stella questioned.

"We are very sure. And he's taunting us. He sent my cousin Sinead, who's also with the FBI, a text message that indicated his next murder would happen on Broadway."

"That's like looking for a needle in a haystack. With all the theaters, the number of employees is astronomical. You've got ushers, actors, concession stand workers…" Her voice trailed as she fathomed the number of potential victims.

"Exactly. Countless blond, blue-eyed men fit the profile, and we were trying to find one whose first name starts with an L."

"Could you search employee records?"

"All the theaters we visited no longer have access to their employee files. The online records have vanished as if someone purposely deleted them."

"And this has happened at more than one theater?"

Brennan nodded. "Multiple. I spoke with the managers, and they are just as baffled. Whoever our killer is, his ability to hack those records tells us he's technically proficient with serious computer skills. He's also making it very hard for us to get ahead of him."

"Wow!" Stella said. "Just wow!"

There was a moment of silence that descended over them. Stella savored a bite of her meal, the decadent seasoning of the sautéed chicken and rice bathed in the creamiest garlic sauce. The meat melted like butter in her mouth, teasing her taste buds.

She hummed her appreciation. "Mmmm! This is delicious!" she said.

Brennan grinned. "Thank you! And I have to tell you, I'm very impressed with your pantry. I thought my own was well stocked, but yours puts mine to shame."

"I like to cook." Stella smiled back.

"Something we have in common."

Silence blanketed their conversation once again as they both ate with gusto, realizing how hungry they were. The day had been long in many ways, and their missed meals hadn't been an issue until good food had been put in front of them.

Stella was swiping a wedge of Italian bread across her plate to catch the last remnants of sauce when Brennan turned the conversation back to business.

"Who needed Rockwell dead and wanted you to go down for the crime?"

She swallowed the last bite of her food and sat back against her seat. "I've been racking my brain to answer that question, and I don't have an answer that makes an ounce of sense."

"How long were you and Rockwell together?"

"We had celebrated our one-year anniversary in the Bahamas a few months ago. He had surprised me with a weekend getaway." The light in Stella's eyes diminished slightly as she began to reflect back on her relationship. "Rockwell and I met when I was doing an article on the proclivity of candidates using fraudulent campaign finances. We had an instant connection. He was sweet and I liked him."

"Sounds like your trip was a good time."

"Not really," Stella said, her eyes shifting across Brennan's face. "That's when Rockwell announced I needed to start being a better partner if I planned to go the distance with him. Those were his exact words. 'If I planned to go the distance with him.'"

She shook her head ever so slightly. "It really was the beginning of the end. I found out that he was letting people think that I was some poor girl from the projects, who'd lived in low-income housing and put herself through school. I know his mother and Tobias had a lot to do with that, but he never did anything to correct the narrative. It infuriated me!"

"He sounds like a jerk!"

Stella shrugged her narrow shoulders. "He was never overly affectionate and was very pedestrian in his approach to life, but when he decided to run for the governor's office, everything revolved around the campaign. Suddenly, I wasn't the woman he loved but the woman who could help him pull in the African

American vote with my rags-to-riches story. Everything I said or did needed to be construed so that it made him look good. I was told how to dress, who I should associate with and how I should behave in public. We began to fight from sunup till sundown, and neither of us were happy. Him telling some donor that I had once worked as a waitress to support myself was the final straw. Had it been true, it wouldn't have been a problem, but it was a blatant lie, and I refused to support his lying to people. I retreated to my corner and cut off contact. I needed space to think things through."

She blew a soft sigh before continuing. "Then last week, he sent me a text message after I refused to show up to an NRA fundraiser, saying that it wasn't working for him anymore. He blocked my number, refused to take my calls and the rest is history."

"Definitely a jerk!"

"He had his moments."

"Did you still love him?"

The quiet between them was suddenly thunderous as she pondered the question. It had been something she'd thought a lot about even before she and Rockwell had gone their separate ways. Their relationship had been a timeline of super highs and super lows. The good times had been some of the best moments she'd ever had. When things went left, she had questioned more than once if they would be able to come back from the fallout. Over the last few months, she had often questioned if the feelings between them had anything at all to do with love.

She sighed again before she answered. "I really cared about Rockwell. When he wasn't trying to live up to other people's expectations, he was really a good guy. Those were our greatest times together, when I was able to see the best of him. Once he took that nosedive into politics, those times became fewer and farther between. Love became an unnecessary commodity for his goals. He just needed me to stand quietly by his side and to smile pretty."

"Would you have married him?"

"I never had any illusions about us having a future together. I think we both always knew that what we shared was only supposed to be momentary," she said. "Does that answer your question?"

"I think I get it," Brennan said softly. He swallowed the last of his beer, depositing the bottle back onto the table. "Rockwell Henley was an even bigger jerk than I gave him credit for, because you clearly are not the trophy wife type."

Stella laughed. "No, I definitely am not."

"Who in Rockwell's inner circle might have had it out for you?"

"I'm fairly certain his parents are on the top of that list. They didn't think I was good enough for their precious son. In fact, when we first got together, his father offered me cash to go away and never see Rockwell again. His mother was just blatantly nasty toward me. To hear her tell it, I am too outspoken, and me working for a *tabloid* newspaper made Rockwell and the family look bad."

"So, we have Ma and Pa Henley. But do you think

either of them actually harbored ill will toward their son to want to see him dead and blame you for it?"

"Not at all. His mother doted on him, and Rockwell idolized his father, fawning over the man every chance he could. His father ate that crap up like expensive caviar."

"Who else? Did Rockwell have any siblings?"

"No. He was an only child. But you can add Tobias Humphrey, his campaign manager, to that list. Tobias is definitely not a member of my fan club."

"What problem did he have with you?"

"To hear him tell it, I added 'negative value' to the campaign. After running a background check on me and trying to dig up whatever dirt he could find, he actually had the audacity to tell Rockwell that dating me was not a good look for a man of his stature. We butted heads every time we ran into each other."

Negative value. Brennan winced. Clearly, Tobias Humphrey had not bothered to know the woman before him. "Do you think he said that because you're black?" he suddenly questioned, unable to shake the thought.

"What do you think?" Stella answered. Her brow lifted as she gave him a look that spoke volumes. She suddenly rose from the table, reaching for the dirty dishes. She moved back into the kitchen to the sink. Brennan's eyes followed as she began to clean up what remained of the mess he'd made.

Brennan felt his body tense, a hint of ire rising in his midsection. His gaze dropped to the table as he contemplated the challenges Stella had been made to endure. The thought that someone had given the woman a hard time for no good reason wasn't sitting right with him. He glanced up as she continued, her voice raised slightly so as to carry the sound through the open door.

"Oh, and let's not forget Miss Rebecca Farrington! Rebecca Farrington of the *South Hampton* Farringtons!" Stella exclaimed sarcastically.

"Who's she?" he questioned as he moved into the kitchen with her. He leaned his elbows on the counter, then rested his head against his closed fists.

"Rockwell's ex-girlfriend. She was livid when he broke up with her, and she had been harboring a lot of animosity toward him. When he and I started dating, she suddenly wanted to reconcile. She has tried everything short of hog-tying him in the basement to get him to come back to her, and nothing had worked. She blamed me for that. To hear her tell it, I had him bewitched."

"Do you think she may have wanted him dead?"

"It was only a few weeks ago that she threatened to kill him."

"Was she serious?"

Stella rolled her eyes skyward. "She said it, that's all I know. And there was enough concern about it that Tobias requested the police go pay her a visit. I'll admit I may have thought it a time or two, but I never said it out loud."

"Please, don't admit that to the prosecutor or any of the detectives working this case!"

Brennan gave her the slightest smile and Stella

smiled back. There was a shift of energy that swept between them, something easy and light. It felt like an old slipper that fit perfectly. It was comfortable, like home.

For a second, he thought about wrapping his arms around her and pulling her close against him. It was an urge he was finding difficult to ignore, desire pulling at him with the force of a freight train. It unnerved him as he felt his entire body quiver with emotion. He took a deep breath, needing to exorcise the thoughts running through his head. "Do you have a computer I can use?" he asked, hopeful for a distraction. He tried to sound calm and collected, but his voice cracked ever so slightly.

Stella's smiled widened even more. She gestured with her head. "Upstairs in my office. It's off the master bedroom. Make yourself at home."

She swiped her hands across a blue plaid dish cloth. Taking a moment to uncork a second bottle of wine, Stella reached for her glass, carrying both as she headed toward the patio and back outside.

As she settled down, lifting her feet onto an ottoman, Brennan didn't take his eyes off her. Wisps of hair had fallen over her eyes. The tension that had been in her face earlier that day was gone, a relaxing glow washing over her. She was breathtaking beneath the setting sun, the last radiant beams spotlighting her delicate features.

"I could get use to this," Brennan muttered to himself as he finally turned and headed up to the second floor of her home.

Chapter 6

Make yourself at home. Clearly, I have lost my mind, Stella thought as she refilled her glass. She sat the bottle of wine on the ground beside her chair. She needed a few minutes to simply unwind, and although she felt relaxed for the first time that day, she was still unsettled by everything that had happened, and Brennan's presence in her home wasn't helping.

She liked him. He wasn't the asshole she'd first figured him for. Although there was still much she didn't know about him, she sensed he was really one of the good guys. And she liked him more than she had ever anticipated.

She had never imagined herself sharing so much about her previous relationship with anyone. But there was a level of comfort with Brennan that was unexpected. He was easy to talk to, and she found herself chattering away like they'd known each other for years. The fact that she had subconsciously given him free rein in her home also spoke volumes. But she was secure about him being in her space, and that had never happened with any man before. Not even with Rockwell Henley.

Brennan followed the exposed brick walls and hardwood floors that carried through to the upper level. On the second story, he found the bright master suite complete with a large walk-in closet and marble-covered bathroom. The decor was minimalistic, with Stella favoring a subtle sage green and light tan. He peeked into the second bedroom, which also had a private bathroom and gorgeous large arched windows. Curious, he ascended the skylit staircase to discover two additional bedrooms with a shared bathroom and walk-in closets. He was duly impressed.

Back on the second floor, he entered the master suite and moved to the office area connected by a sliding barn door. The desk inside hosted a Mac computer and a picture of Stella and her parents. She'd been young, wearing bell-bottom jeans, large framed glasses and an oversized afro. Her distinguished parents were dressed in their Sunday best. They looked happy, and he imagined it was a memory that was near and dear to Stella's heart.

If she actually worked in that office, he would never have known it. Like the rest of her home, the space was immaculate. If he'd been trying to discover what she was working on, he would have been challenged. There was no evidence of anything but her having hired a really great cleaning company.

Brennan liked Stella. He liked her a lot. He was enjoying himself so much that for the briefest moment, he forgot that he was there to solve a crime. His time with her wasn't meant to be personal. It needed to be all business. But she was making that harder than it needed to be. She was proving herself to be quite the distraction. And he was putting the blame on her because…well…why not? Admitting she had him completely smitten didn't fit his image. And it wasn't going to help them find the bad guys. Blaming her helped him rationalize his own shortcomings. Putting the onus on Stella helped him not feel bad about being distracted if she were to blame.

He closed his eyes as he waited for her computer to turn on. There was no password, and he bypassed the screen saver picture with the push of the Enter button. That she had given him permission to use the device and access that didn't require her looking over his shoulder said much about her level of comfort with him in her space. He respected that and knew he'd do nothing to lose her trust. They were becoming fast friends and because he didn't have many people that he himself trusted, he didn't want to mess things up between them.

After weeding through his email, Brennan called his cousin to check in. Rory answered on the second ring.

"Where are you?" she questioned, not even bothering to say hello.

"At Stella Maxwell's home."

"Is she okay?"

"I think so. Did you get anything on that van?"

"It was stolen a few hours earlier. They ditched it a few miles from the station, leaving it in a parking garage. It had been wiped clean."

Brennan heaved a deep sigh. "That's not a lot of help."

"No, it isn't," Rory replied. "Have you been able to come up with anything?"

"Nothing. But something about this case isn't sitting right with me," Brennan said. "Why would someone try to set Stella up and then try to snatch her? Assuming both were connected."

"Do you think they're not?"

"I'm not sure what I think. We have more questions than we do answers. Starting with how someone knew she'd be released in order to be outside waiting for her?"

"What are you thinking?"

"How well do you know everyone on your team?" Brennan questioned.

There was a moment of hesitation before Rory responded. "How well do you know everyone on yours? Even if you are related to most of them."

"My point precisely. It's possible our perp is working with someone in the department. Someone privy to Stella's case. Someone able to pass along information about her comings and goings. Someone neither of us would suspect, because we think we know them, and we really don't know them all as well as we think we do."

"You seem pretty certain that this is all about Stella and not Rockwell Henley, the victim."

"I think setting her up and then going after her puts a spotlight on Stella. Think about it. If I wanted Henley dead, I would have just killed him. Why go through the trouble of setting Stella up to take the fall, unless my grudge was against her, and Henley was just a means to an end. I think he was collateral damage. And I think whoever did it isn't finished. Them trying to grab her this afternoon says that."

"Unfortunately, if your theory is true, we don't have the man power to give her twenty-four-hour protection. Hell, we barely have enough men to investigate the murder. Between budget cuts and staff shortages, we are stretched thin."

"Don't worry about it. I'm not going anywhere."

"What about the Landmark Killer case? You certain Sergeant Blackthorn won't have an issue with you shifting your focus? He already had issues with the FBI team working the case anyway."

Brennan thought about Sergeant Wells Blackthorn. He was the lead on the Landmark Killer case, reporting to the precinct captain, Colleen Reeves, who had called in Brennan's team to help with the case. They were a specialized unit of the Manhattan FBI and brought a unique perspective to their work.

Wells didn't like that the FBI was involved, although the team was full of experts who specialized in serial killers. It included Brennan; his cousin, Special Agent Sinead Colton; his twin brother, Special Agent Cash Colton; his sister, Agent Ashlyn Colton, who was their technical expert and his brother Patrick Colton, an FBI CSI expert.

Brennan's cousin Sinead and Sergeant Blackthorn had bumped heads hard in the beginning, both wanting to go it alone. Despite the tension between them, the duo had grown close, soon bumping other body parts that Brennan chose not to think about. He was happy for Sinead and grateful she'd been able to find love and a modicum of happiness in the midst of so much darkness.

"I'll talk to him," Brennan said. "I can work both cases. It'll be okay."

Brennan could just imagine his cousin's expression. He hadn't sounded so convincing, and he had no doubts she too had reservations. He shifted the conversation.

"I'll keep my eyes on Ms. Maxwell."

"Well, the NYPD appreciates your assistance. As long as you don't get in our way."

"What have your guys done thus far?" Brennan queried.

"My men have talked to Henley's friends and his family. We've also spoken to his political opponent. Most of those interviews pointed back to Stella and their relationship ending on bad terms. She's been described as a woman scorned. To hear them tell it, everyone else loved him. He was a great guy and Stella was the problem."

Brennan shook his head. He blew a soft sigh, realizing he was faced with another case that would prove to be an uphill battle.

"If you turn up anything, let me know," he said.

"You do the same," Rory responded. "And be safe, please."

Brennan smiled into the receiver as if she could see him. "Yeah, yeah," he answered.

Stella woke with a start. She hadn't planned to doze off sitting out in the garden, but the warm late-night air had pulled her into the sweetest slumber. Gathering her bearings, she sat upright and shifted her body forward in the seat. Filling her lungs with a deep inhale of air, her eyes darted back and forth across the landscape. It only took a quick minute for her to remember the hard day that she'd had. Her heart was still reeling over the murder of Rockwell, and remembering that someone had tried to cause her harm cramped her stomach with fear. Then she remembered that her hard day had ended with an air of hope and a man making himself comfortable in her home. A man who'd seemingly disappeared since climbing the stairs to her second floor.

She rose from her seat and headed inside, securing the door behind her. The stereo was still playing, the softest jazz billowing out of the built-in speakers throughout the house. She dropped her wine glass and the empty bottle of Moscato into the kitchen sink, then headed upstairs to her bedroom.

She saw Brennan from the top of the stairwell. She

paused to stare into her bedroom. He too had given in to the exhaustion that had hit like a tidal wave. He'd sat down at the foot of her bed and had fallen asleep. His feet were still planted firmly on the floor, but he'd fallen over on his side, his torso lying awkwardly atop the mattress. He snored loudly, and Stella sensed it had been some time since he'd slept so soundly. The sight of him made her smile.

Easing her way back down the staircase, she checked the locks on her front door one last time, peering out the sidelights to the street. All was quiet, nothing seeming amiss. She stared out into the darkness for a good few minutes, rehashing everything that happened one more time. Despite being hopeful that things might go back to normal after a good night's sleep, she instinctively knew normal wouldn't be visiting her anytime soon. With a deep sigh, she settled herself down against the sofa. Pulling a light cotton blanket over her legs, she drifted back to sleep with thoughts of Brennan Colton still spinning in her mind.

The smell of freshly brewed coffee pulled Stella from a deep slumber. The sound of pots rattling was startling, and her heart was suddenly racing. She sat upright, unaccustomed to the sounds and aromas wakening her from her sleep. She started to reach for the baseball bat she kept hidden beneath the sofa when a booming voice called her name.

"Good morning! I was starting to wonder if you

were going to get up or if I was going to have to wake you." Brennan Colton grinned broadly.

Stella found his cheerful expression off-putting, considering her side and back ached from sleeping on the sofa. She needed time to stretch and loosen those muscles and a moment to whisper a quiet prayer skyward before having to face the world. She winced as he called her name a second time.

"Are you okay, Stella?" Brennan questioned.

"I'm fine. Why are you so damn chipper?" she asked. She tossed off the blanket wrapped around her and slid her feet to the floor. With a wide yawn, she stretched her arms skyward, then twisted her head from side to side.

"It's going to be a good day," he responded. "I can feel it!"

"Well, I can't," Stella snapped.

"Coffee will help. How do you take yours?"

"Black," she said.

Brennan nodded and disappeared back into her kitchen. He returned minutes later with an oversized mug filled with a rich blend of Columbian coffee beans. At the first sip, Stella felt her mood shift. She closed her eyes and settled into the comfort of the hot brew.

"Mmmm," she purred. "Okay, this is good." She hummed her appreciation a second time. "So why are you up so early?" she asked. "And where'd you get the suit?"

It had taken her a moment to notice that Brennan was wearing a clean change of clothes, his outfit from the previous day replaced by a navy silk suit, white dress shirt and red paisley necktie. He'd shaved, no hint of morning stubble on his face. The waves in his blond hair lay pristinely atop his head, and his blue eyes shimmered with excitement.

Brennan chuckled. "One, it's not early. It's almost one o'clock in the afternoon. And two, while you were asleep, I went home to shower and change. I borrowed your keys to let myself back in. You were sleeping so soundly that I didn't want to wake you. You looked like you needed the rest."

Eyes wide, Stella stole a quick glance at the watch on her wrist. She was suddenly feeling out of sorts again knowing he'd gone and come back, and she hadn't heard a thing. That most of the day had already passed her by without her accomplishing a thing felt wrong on many levels. She jumped from seat still holding tight to her coffee mug.

"I need to change," she muttered. "I need to…"

Brennan interrupted her. "You need to come and get something to eat. Then you need to just rest. I don't want you leaving the house. We still don't know who came after you, and I don't know that it's safe. I need you to be safe."

"Did they get anything on that van?"

Brennan shook his head. "They hit a dead end. Which is why you need to stay low until we have more. All of this feels very personal, and I think there's someone coming after you. Maybe because of Henley, or maybe he was just a casualty of the war being waged against you. I don't know which, but I do know I don't want anything to happen to you."

Brennan's eyes were piercing as he stared at her. Stella felt her face flush, a wave of heat flooding her from her head down to her toes. She wasn't sure how to respond, having nothing to say that would have made sense. She shook her head, her eyes darting around the room so to not meet his.

"What are you cooking?" she finally questioned.

Brennan smiled. "Breakfast casserole. I'm warming up a slice for you. There's also some fresh fruit: grapes, mandarin oranges, watermelon, cherries and some blueberries. I stopped by the grocery store on my way back."

Stella's eyes widened again, and her stomach rumbled at the thought of food. She moved in his direction, following him into the kitchen. He pointed her to the counter.

"Did anyone tell you that you're bossy?" Stella said as she moved onto one of the bar stools.

Brennan shrugged. "I've been called a few things over the years, but I don't know if *bossy* was one of them."

He gave her a smile as he set a plate of food down in front of her. Stella hesitated before starting to eat, watching him as he put everything away. She wasn't sure how she felt about him being so in control in her space. What irked her most is that he didn't bother her as much as she would have imagined just days earlier.

"I need to run," Brennan said. "I have an appointment with Rockwell's family, and I want to catch up with his campaign manager. I'll be back later this evening."

"I should go with you."

Brennan pointed his index finger in her direction. "Do not leave this house, Stella. I mean that. I can't be certain it's safe for you out there alone."

"I won't be alone if I'm with you," she snapped back.

He shook his head. "That's not possible. And I need you to work with me on this. Please."

Stella narrowed her eyes significantly, like thin slits of hostility and anger. Her face reddened beneath the warm brown of her complexion, her cheeks heated and bulging as she clenched her teeth tightly together. Words were lost to her, a lengthy list of profanity flying from her thoughts. She wanted to curse him, but the energy wasn't there either. Instead, she blew a soft sigh and shoved a spoonful of baked eggs, cheese, mushrooms, onions and bacon into her mouth.

As Brennan moved past her, he rested a large hand on her shoulder and squeezed it gently. "I'll be back a few hours," he said.

"You plan on staying another night?" she questioned.

"I'm here every night until we find who's after you. Is that going to be a problem?"

Stella shrugged. "Just stay in the guest room. I like my own bed."

He grinned. "I liked your bed too. It's very comfortable! I appreciate you not throwing me out of it, because I slept very well last night."

There was a hint of amusement in his tone. And

innuendo, as if he wanted to say the only thing that would have been better was if she had been in that bed with him. Or maybe, Stella thought, she was imagining that part, and those thoughts were her own.

Brennan squeezed her shoulder a second time and then headed out the door. As he disappeared through the entrance, that lengthy list of profanity came back to her, and Stella cursed out loud.

Chapter 7

Brennan was early for his appointment with Dayn and Silvia Henley, the parents of the late Rockwell Henley. He was met at the door of their West 57th Street apartment by a doorman who was all brawn and minimal brain. His gray uniform looked two sizes too small, his muscles bulging through the cotton fabric. His voice was nasally, sounding like he needed a tissue to clear his sinuses. He was intimidating, until he talked, his voice giving playful helium balloon vibes.

He looked Brennan up and then down before informing him that the Henleys were not ready to see him, and he would have to wait in the lobby for their okay to send him up to the penthouse.

Brennan gave his watch a quick glance. "Can you

let them know this won't take long? I understand they have someplace to be and so do I."

The doorman simply stared. Clearly, he was not going to be moved. With nowhere for Brennan to sit, he moved to the other side of the room and leaned against the marbled wall. The doorman cleared his throat as though he wanted to say something, but he bit back the comment; instead, pausing to sign for a package for another tenant.

Time dragged ever so slowly. Ten minutes passed before the doorman gestured for Brennan's attention. He pointed him toward the elevator. "The Henleys will see you now," he said.

Brennan sighed as he stepped into the conveyor, the doors closing after him. The elevator moved swiftly, the ride so smooth that it barely felt as if he'd left the first floor. When the doors opened, he was standing in the Henleys' living room, the couple meeting him at the entrance.

Dayn Henley stepped forward, his hand extended. He looked like old money, Brennan thought. He was nicely tanned, his complexion boosting weekly skin care treatments done by a professional. His gray hair had been neatly combed, a slight wave to the thick strands. He wore a short-sleeve, polo-style shirt with his initials embroidered on the pocket and tailored black slacks. He exuded confidence, an aura of conviction and determination wafting off him. Under different circumstances, he and Brennan would probably have liked each other.

His wife held court behind him, not budging from

where she stood. Her hands were folded politely in front of the short, plaid skirt she wore. She stood on stiletto heels that complemented toned legs that said strip club, not country club. Her blonde hair was thick and lush with just the barest hint of a curl, and she wore enough makeup for three women. Brennan instinctively knew she would never like him, and he didn't see himself caring much about her.

"We'll need to make this quick, Agent Colton," Dayn Kenley said. "My son's law firm is holding a small community vigil later today to honor him."

"Do you have any new leads?" Mrs. Kenley interjected. "Do you know who helped that woman kill our son?"

"We have our best men investigating your son's murder. I just have a few questions for you."

Mrs. Kenley rolled her eyes skyward, annoyance furrowing her brow. "We've answered more than enough questions. It's time we got some answers. Have you spoken with that woman?"

"And what woman might that be?" Brennan asked, already knowing the answer.

"Stella Maxwell!" the older woman spat. "Our son was associated with her briefly. He recently ended the relationship, and she didn't take it well. I wouldn't be surprised if you discover that she is somehow responsible."

"It's my understanding that Rockwell and Stella dated for over a year. That would be a little more than a brief association, wouldn't you say?"

Silvia Kenley rolled her eyes again. "Their relationship was done and finished, that's all that matters."

Dayn shot his wife a look before shifting his gaze back toward Brennan. "They were very good friends, Stella and Rockwell. He cared for her very much, but they had very different life goals."

"Do you think she was involved in your son's murder?"

"I think their relationship ended on bad terms and we never know what we'll do if we're pushed too far."

"So, you think Rockwell pushed Stella to her breaking point?"

"Stella could be difficult," Silvia interjected. "And mean-spirited. People like her can be dangerous."

"People like her?"

"Do you have any more questions, Agent Colton?" Dayn asked. He stepped in front of his wife, quietly silencing anything else she might have had to say. She turned abruptly, scurrying from the room in a huff.

"Do you know of anyone else who might have had a grudge against your son?" Brennan asked.

Dayn shook his head. "If you've spoken with anyone from his law firm, you know he was very well-respected."

"He practiced corporate law, is that correct?"

"Yes, and he was well-liked by the companies he represented. Since he never practiced criminal law, he never made any enemies that we know of. Rockwell was very much a people person. Everyone liked him. It's what made him a great political candidate."

"Do you think Stella Maxwell was involved in your son's death, Mr. Henley?"

The patriarch shook his head. "No, I don't. Stella made my son happy. She cared about Rockwell. But his political ambitions and his mother's influence didn't serve their relationship well."

"Thank you," Brennan said. "I appreciate you taking time to speak with me."

"Find my son's killer, Agent."

"I'm doing everything we can, sir."

"Well, do more!" Silvia snapped from the doorway.

Both men turned toward her, noting the look of disgust on her face. She was not a happy woman and Brennan imagined her unhappiness had made her son, and Stella, miserable. With one last nod of his head, he stepped back into the elevator, the two men still eyeing each other before the doors closed and the conveyor returned to the first floor.

The campaign office of Rockwell Henley for Governor was deserted. When Brennan stepped through the doors, he hadn't known what he'd find. But he didn't expect it to be quite so desolate. Any evidence of a campaign being waged no longer existed, everything packed up or tossed away. Something about the space felt out of sorts, feeling as if all traces of Rockwell Henley had been erased in the twenty-four hours since he had died.

"Hello?" He called out, noise coming from someplace in the rear of the building. "Is anyone here?"

The noise stopped but no one appeared. The quiet

was slightly disconcerting. Brennan called out a second time, his hand moving to the gun holstered beneath his arm. "Hello? Is anyone here?"

"Yes, hello!" A young woman suddenly rushed forward. A wide, gummy smile pulled across her face. Her thin lips showcased a mouth full of picture-perfect teeth resulting from years of orthodontic and periodontal work. Mousy brown hair framed nondescript facial features and hazel eyes that were flecked with gold. She had beautiful eyes, with lengthy lashes that she batted easily when necessary. Brennan found himself staring at her eyes, those flecks of gold shimmering in the light.

She was slim, but not overly thin, nor did she have a figure that garnered second looks. She wasn't homely, nor was she outrageously beautiful. She was plain, and average in appearance with the bubbliest of personalities to make up for whatever she thought her physical shortcomings might be.

Her arms were wrapped tightly around her torso as she moved toward him. "May I help you?"

"Yes, hello." Brennan flashed his badge at her. "I'm with the FBI and I was hoping to speak with Tobias Humphrey. My name is Colton. Special agent Brennan Colton."

"Is this about Rockwell?"

"I just need to ask Mr. Humphrey a few questions," he said with a slight nod.

The young woman sighed, her hand brushing the length of her hair from her face. "It's just so horrible!" She suddenly started crying, tears raining over her cheeks. "We loved him so much!"

Brennan nodded, caught off guard by her water-works. "And you are?"

She swiped at her eyes with the back of her hand. "Pamela. Pamela Littlefield. I'm Mr. Humphrey's personal assistant." The tears stopped as quickly as they'd started.

"Is Mr. Humphrey available or do you know how I might reach him?"

The woman named Pamela shook her head. "He's not here. He may be with the Henley family. They were all very close."

Brennan nodded. "I imagine you knew Mr. Henley well. Have you been with the campaign since the beginning?"

"Yes. I've worked for Mr. Humphrey for years. And I knew Rockwell from school. It turned out to be a great partnership. Until…well…" The tears started again.

"Is there anything you can tell me about Mr. Henley? Anything that might explain someone wanting to kill him?"

Pamela shook her head. "No, not really. Everyone loved Rockwell." She pulled a hand to her chest, manicured fingers tapping lightly at that dip between her sterna. "He was such a generous man and so kind. People were drawn to him. I didn't know anyone who didn't love everything about him. Everyone except, maybe, Stella Maxwell." There was a sudden edge to her voice as she mentioned Stella's name.

"Stella Maxwell? You know Stella?"

She nodded. "Stella and Rockwell dated, but it

didn't work out. His mother didn't care for her. Stella wasn't overly supportive of Rockwell's political aspirations. It was a huge problem between them. They fought all the time. It started to affect the campaign, so he broke it off with her. Tobias felt that was for the best. I heard she didn't take it well."

"And where did you hear that?" Brennan questioned.

"His mother. I heard Mrs. Henley tell Tobias that Stella really went after Rockwell. She said she sent him some hateful messages. Threatening him and such. Apparently, it was bad."

Brennan listened as she regaled him with a lengthy list of Stella's wrongdoings. Things that had irritated his mother or annoyed the campaign manager. It was apparent that short of walking on water, there was nothing Stella could have done that would have impressed any of them. From all the woman shared, the only individual who didn't complain about Stella had been Rockwell. Rockwell, who'd neither defended her nor castigated her, but seemed hopeful that if he ignored the peanut gallery tossing their two cents in on his relationship, it would work itself out. When it hadn't, he'd given in to the pressure.

Pamela shook her head from side to side. "That's what I heard, but I don't know how true it is, of course."

"Do you think Ms. Maxwell had something to do with Mr. Henley's murder?"

There was a lengthy pause before the woman answered. "Rockwell's mother thought she was problematic. Tobias didn't have good things to say about her either. But I honestly don't know her well enough to say if she was capable of murder or not. She was always very nice to me. I liked her. Had she been around longer, I think we would have been good friends."

"One last question," Brennan said. "Where were you yesterday morning between nine and eleven o'clock?"

"Me?" Her voice cracked as if the question surprised her. "I was here, closing down the office," she said as she gestured behind her with an open palm.

"Can anyone confirm that?" Brennan asked.

Pamela shrugged her narrow shoulders. "I'm sure Mr. Humphrey can verify my whereabouts. He was here too. On the phone mostly."

Brennan pulled a business card from the inner pocket of his suit jacket. "Would you please have Mr. Humphrey give me a call when he has an opportunity? It's important that I speak with him."

Pamela took the card from his hand. "I will. And if I think of anything that might be important, I'll make sure to contact you."

"Thank you for your time, Ms. Littlefield."

"It was my pleasure," Pamela said, tossing in one last sniffle before that wide smile returned.

Out on the sidewalk, Brennan could feel Pamela Littlefield still staring at him. When he turned around to look, she was closing the thin white blinds that covered the windows, disappearing from view. She was what his mother would call an odd bird, he thought, although he found her friendly enough. She was one of those people who seemed almost too eager to be helpful and that never boded well with Brennan. People like that always made him wary. He made a mental note to ask Stella about the woman. He was curious to know her opinion of the personal assistant who would have been besties with her in another life.

Thus far, the general consensus from those he'd spoken with, was that Stella was evil incarnate. They presumed she could projectile vomit, eat small children and castrate the male species on a whim. Most wanted her to be guilty of Rockwell Henley's murder. He imagined that once they learned she had an alibi and was innocent, they would still choose to believe that she was somehow involved.

Brennan checked the time, adjusting the watch on his wrist. He planned to show up at Rockwell's memorial, standing in the back to watch the crowd. He also hoped to have a conversation with the ex-girlfriend who Stella claimed wanted to reconcile with Rockwell. Before then though he needed to see where the local police were with the Landmark Killer case. He hadn't heard anything, which told him they hadn't been successful in their search for the next potential victim. He was starting to feel like that case was going nowhere fast. He didn't want to admit that they might not be able to stop the killer from dropping another body into their laps.

* * *

Stella found everything she needed to know on her computer. She had never unsubscribed from Rockwell's campaign newsletter and news of his death had come just hours after his body had been found. Shortly after there was an announcement about a vigil being hosted by his law firm, campaign team and his parents. It included the date, time and address, and only gave her a few short hours to get ready and get there. They planned a private funeral for family only, later in the week.

She thought about Brennan's admonishments for her to stay put, but following directions had never been her strong suit. Not even as a child. Stella had always done things her own way no matter the consequences. She needed to be at this memorial. If for no other reason to show the naysayers that she hadn't killed Rockwell and she wasn't afraid of whoever might be coming after her. That was, of course, a lie. She was scared to death, but she refused to let it get the best of her. She also knew that not going made her look guilty. She'd be damned before she allowed them to whisper behind her back about killing the man. She'd done no such thing and she intended to say so. And not even the likes of Brennan Colton, was going to stop her.

Hours later, Stella was showered and primped, her hair pulled up into a neat bun, and her makeup meticulous. She'd chosen a black silk tank dress with a matching duster coat. The dress material was form-fitting and the long-sleeved duster lightweight enough for the warm weather. With just the hint of a black heel, she looked polished and professional, like the grieving ex-girlfriend of a New York politician.

Staring at her reflection in the mirror, Stella suddenly kicked off the black heels. She searched the bottom of her closet until she found the perfect pair of shoes; a pair of vintage, Dolce & Gabbana, lime green alligator pumps that Rockwell had gifted to her for her birthday the previous year. With one final glance in the mirror, she felt more like herself, still polished and professional but not nearly as stifling and cold as Rockwell's family and friends would have liked. Lime green had been Rockwell's favorite color.

Hours later, Stella was traveling to the Upper East Side, taking the subway from 125th Street to 86th Street. From there, she walked to Pratt Mansions on Fifth Avenue. She took her time, moving casually to her destination, refusing to be overheated and sweaty when she arrived.

As she turned the corner onto Fifth Avenue, Pratt was on one side facing the grandeur of the Metropolitan Museum on the other. She smiled at the sight of the stonework that decorated the outside of the building. She'd attended a wedding or two at that location and always marveled at the beautifully detailed marble and woodwork inside. Rockwell had announced his candidacy there months earlier, so it was fitting that his parents had chosen the space to bid him farewell.

Stella paused on the sidewalk watching as mourners trickled into the building. It was a cornucopia of the city's elite making an appearance. News crews were posted around the building, snapping photos of those who were coming and going. Everyone who wanted to be seen paused long enough at the entrance to have their picture taken. Many of the sad faces and tears were disingenuous, most not even knowing Rockwell personally. Stella had no doubts his mother was duly pleased with the turnout and the displays of emotion for her son. Minutes passed as she gathered her nerves. When she had sufficiently collected her thoughts, Stella took a deep breath, crossed the street and headed inside.

Brennan had been one of the first to arrive to pay their respects to the Henley family for their loss. Mr. Henley had given him the barest of smiles and quick nod of his head, before turning back to the conversation he was having. Mrs. Henley had bristled, clearly displeased with his presence. She whispered hurriedly to the man standing before her, then gave him and Brennan her back. That man came rushing in his direction, his hand extended in greeting.

"Special Agent Colton! Tobias Humphrey," he said, as he grasped Brennan's hand and shook it quickly.

"Mr. Humphrey, it's a pleasure. Thank you for a moment of your time."

Tobias stole a quick glance toward his watch. "And I only have a quick moment. I'm sure you understand."

"I do and I won't intrude any longer than necessary."

Tobias nodded again. He was a small man with even smaller features. He was balding and had taken to combing the last strands of hair holding on across the top of his head from one ear to the other. He wore an expensive silk suit that had been tailored to his stature and leather shoes that would have been a year's salary for Brennan.

"When was the last time you spoke with Rockwell?" Brennan asked.

Tobias sighed. "We were talking the morning he died. He said he had an appointment to keep and that he would meet me at campaign headquarters when he was finished. I asked him what the appointment was for, and he said he was meeting Stella Maxwell at her office to talk. I expressed that I didn't think that was a good idea. They had recently broken up and she hadn't taken it well. Obviously, I was concerned about the optics if she'd intended to publicly embarrass him. He wasn't at all concerned. Clearly, we both should have been."

Tobias pressed a hand to his chest and shook his head vehemently. He continued. "I feel very guilty. I should have insisted he not go, or that I go with him. He might still be here with us if I had."

"Or you might be dead too," Brennan said matter-of-factly.

The man's eyes widened. He suddenly fanned his hand in front of his face as if he could wave that thought away. "Well," he said, "we're grateful that the NYPD were able to make a quick arrest. Them catching her in the act means justice can be served swiftly and without prejudice."

"If she were guilty," Brennan said nonchalantly.

"They caught her in the act!" Tobias repeated. His voice rose slightly, and he took a quick glance around the room to see if anyone had heard. He steadied himself, taking a deep breath, and brushing his hand down the front of his suit jacket.

Brennan didn't bother to tell him that Stella had been proven innocent and released. "Is there anyone else that may have wanted Rockwell dead?" he questioned.

"Not at all. He was well-respected. And very affable. He didn't have any enemies that we were aware of."

"And the party didn't find anything concerning before giving him their support?"

"Nothing, and he had been fully vetted."

"It's my understanding that you recently reported some concerns with a young woman named Rebecca Farrington. I understand she and Rockwell had dated before he and Ms. Maxwell were together?"

"It's campaign policy to report any threats made against our candidates. Rebecca was brokenhearted and said some heated things in a moment of passion. She was very apologetic, and the police found nothing credible to be concerned about. In fact," he said, gesturing toward the Henley family who stood at the front of the room by an oversized, framed photo of their son. "Rebecca has been by the family's side supporting them since the news broke."

Brennan looked to where he pointed. The young woman standing beside Rockwell's mother was quite a beauty. Long and lean, she flipped the length of her brunette hair with severe blond highlights over her shoulder. She wore a tailored, pale blue pant suit. There was a single button holding it closed and with the hint of cleavage showing, Brennan fathomed there wasn't much beneath it. She looked quite comfortable with her hand holding tightly onto Mrs. Henley's elbow.

He turned his attention back to Tobias. "Did Stella Maxwell ever make any threats that campaign policy dictated you report? Any threats against Mr. Henley's life that were concerning enough for the police to become involved?"

Brennan felt the man bristle, a hint of indignation washing over his expression. He pulled at the collar of his shirt, adjusting his necktie. "No, not that I was ever made aware of," he finally muttered.

"Can anyone verify your whereabouts yesterday morning, Mr. Humphrey?"

The man paused as if he needed to think about it. "I was at campaign headquarters until I came here to meet with the caterer and the venue manager. My assistant saw me there and multiple people saw me here."

Brennan stared at the man before finally extending his hand. "Thank you again for your time, Mr. Humphrey. I plan to stay a while longer. I promise not to get in the way."

The two men shook hands one last time before Tobias turned and scurried to the other side of the room.

Moving to the rear of the spacious event hall, Brennan positioned himself against the back wall. His arms were crossed over his chest as his eyes darted back and forth, taking it all in. People were steadily filing in and soon, most of the chairs were filled, everyone waiting for the speech to begin.

He kept his eye on Rebecca, who continued to stand with the family. She'd made hair flipping an art form. Every other comment or gesture included a toss of her lengthy strands. There was a brief exchange between her and Tobias, the two seeming unhappy with each other. She displayed classic, mean girl attitude, dismissive of those she considered beneath her.

Brennan had also done the requisite Google search on Miss Farrington. She too had come from money; the oldest daughter born to a plastic surgeon father and orthodontist mother. She and Rockwell had gone to school together. They'd been college sweethearts betrothed to each other on graduation day. The engagement had ended when she'd left Rockwell for a New York Giants football player with a five-year, multi-million-dollar contract. That relationship ended when the football player injured his back, his career cut short.

Rebecca was also a former Miss New York contestant, placing in the top twenty-five the first year she competed, and the top ten her second year. The verdict was still out on whether she'd compete a third time. She relied heavily on her looks and only because they often took her far. She was very much a younger version of Rockwell's mother in demeanor, the two women cut from the same angry burlap cloth. Brennan had dated many women like her. More than his fair share if he were honest. Pretty packages with

questionable content. Without exchanging one word
with the woman, he understood why Rockwell had
shown no interest in a reconciliation and why his parents had considered her perfect trophy wife material.

Eyeing the who's who of New York as they pan-
dered to one another was proving to be both boring
and entertaining, on the same level as bird-watching,
Brennan thought to himself. There was no one who
stood out, looking like they may have killed the man
everyone was there to honor.

Pamela Littlejohn flitted about anxiously, trying
to make herself useful. She followed after Tobias,
ready to fulfill any order before he even needed to
make a request of her. She wore the same bright smile
she'd greeted Brennan with earlier, peppered with
the same glassy tears that occasionally damped her
lashes. She'd changed into a less stylish black dress
that stopped just below her knees. The youthful Peter
Pan collar was fitting and would have been almost in-
fantile on any other woman. She'd waved at Brennan
excitedly, her exuberance as if they were old friends.
He waved back, thinking that building a rapport with
the young woman might be to his advantage. Her ea-
gerness might be useful as he continued to search out
information.

Brennan's brow lifted ever so slightly when his
cousin Rory entered the room. She'd come dressed for
the occasion, attired in her requisite dark suit, white
blouse, brass badge on her hip and her government-
issued weapon secured in the holster beneath her arm.

He and his cousin exchanged a look, their gazes meeting at the same times.

Rory eased her way to his side and greeted him warmly. "What the hell are you doing here?" she asked. "I thought you were keeping your eye on Ms. Maxwell?"

Brennan shrugged. "She's safe at home. I thought I'd do just a little reconnaissance work. I figured this would be a good place to check out potential suspects."

His cousin shook her head. "Did you come up with anything?"

"Not really," he replied. "Everyone here loved Rockwell. He was the golden boy, well-liked, respected, with nary an enemy."

"Except the person who stabbed him," Rory countered. "Anyone have any thoughts on that?"

"All fingers point to Stella. I don't think she has a single friend in this room. The general consensus is she did it."

"Were you expecting different?"

"Not really. I was just hoping something, or someone, would have surprised me."

There was a moment's pause. Then Rory chuckled. "Humph!" she muttered. "It looks like your prayers have been answered." She pointed him toward the door.

Looking over, a wave of shock crossed Brennan's face. His stomach suddenly felt like it was doing a gymnastic floor routine; a back handspring, somersault, two cartwheels, a scissor leap and then a round-off. His breath caught deep in his chest and his mouth was dry. Because Stella stood in the entrance, her gaze locked on the front of the room. She was stunning, looking regal, poised and ready to take on the world.

Chapter 8

Stella had no idea what she expected when she made the decision to show up for Rockwell's memorial service. What she hadn't expected when she moved to the front of the room to offer her condolences to Rockwell's parents was the bloodcurdling scream from Rockwell's mother. It was loud and guttural, pulled from somewhere deep in the matriarch's midsection, and it brought the entire room to a standstill.

"Murderer!" Mrs. Henley cried out, spitting the word in Stella's face. "How dare you show up here! Murderer!"

The chaos that ensued was something straight off the WorldStar video blog. Cameras were flashing, people were shouting, and all Stella could hear was Silvia screeching and Dayn trying to calm her down.

She was suddenly aware of Tobias grabbing her arm and shouting in her ear that she needed to leave, and then Rebecca pushed her way forward, her arm raised high as if to slap Stella's face. Stella braced herself, her fists clenched as she readied herself to strike the woman back and then Brennan stepped between them, wrapping both his arms around her as he gently pushed her back toward the door.

They were blocks away, having crossed over and dipped into Central Park when Brennan finally came to a halt, satisfied that no one had followed them. It was only then, his arms still wrapped protectively around her, that Stella realized she was crying. She turned, leaning into his chest as she sobbed. Brennan continued to hold her, allowing her to release the hurt and pain she'd been holding on to with an iron grip, refusing to allow herself a moment of weakness that anyone could see. He hated to see her this way, wishing that he could do something, anything, to ease the pain she was going through. And then, as if she read his mind, she pulled herself from him, digging into her purse for a tissue.

He shook his head. "I thought I told you to stay put. What were you trying to accomplish?"

"I wanted to pay my respects to the family."

His head was still waving from side to side. "We should have discussed that first."

Stella bristled. "Why haven't you told them that it wasn't me? That I didn't kill their son?"

"We were hoping the real killer would get comfortable. If you looked good for the crime, then they might let their guard down and get sloppy. But I'm sure they know by now," Brennan answered. "I have no doubts Detective Colton told them after that display. But it doesn't mean they're going to welcome you back with open arms, Stella."

"I don't need them to welcome me back. I need them to not look at me like I'm the Antichrist!"

"You don't need them to validate you!"

"No, I don't, but I deserve to have them respect me. That's all. I have not earned the level of disrespect that they continue to show me."

"And what happens if you never change their opinion? If they still dislike you?"

"Nothing happens. I just go on with my life."

Brennan nodded. His voice dropped to a loud whisper. "Baby, it's time for you to move on," he said softly. He reached for her again, pulling her against him.

Stella settled into the warmth, his words washing over her ears in a heated wave. He'd only said what she'd been feeling for months. What she'd resigned herself to when the Henleys had first voiced their displeasure with their son's relationship. What she had always known deep in her heart but had still hoped to change.

She stared down to the green shoes on her feet. A dark stain blemished the left toe, the smudge trailing along the outer edge toward the heel. She blew a heavy sigh as she grabbed Brennan's arm for support. She stepped out of the high-heeled pumps, retrieving a pair of foldable walking shoes from her purse. She pushed her foot into the lightweight slip-on, then bent down to retrieve her designer shoes. She eased over to a wooden bench and rested the shoes on top.

Brennan eyed her curiously. "Those look like a nice pair of shoes. You're just going to leave them?"

Stella nodded. She couldn't begin to explain to Brennan, but she was past ready to kick them and the memories of Rockwell Henley to the curb. "I'm ready to go home," she said softly.

With a nod, Brennan turned, guiding them back in the direction they'd just run from. Neither spoke, and it was just as they exited the park that Stella realized he'd called her baby with all the affection and commitment of a man who genuinely cared about her.

Baby. He'd called her baby. *Baby!* And it had come as naturally to him as breathing. Clearly, Brennan thought, he had officially lost his mind. He'd had no business calling the primary witness in a murder case that he was investigating *baby.* If any of his team found out, he'd be snatched off the case so fast his head would spin. He needed to apologize to Stella. He couldn't blame her if she filed a complaint with his superiors. He had overstepped the professional boundaries of his position, something he had never done in his entire career.

He threw his body back against the mattress of the king-sized bed. When they'd gotten back, Stella had disappeared up the stairs, not bothering to return. As the sun had set, the evening air cooling comfortably, he'd climbed up to the second floor hoping they might have a conversation. He found her bedroom door closed, so he'd stood in the hallway, respecting her desire to be alone. It killed him not to check that she was okay, but he heard her moving about, so he let her be until she was ready to talk to him.

Moving into her spare bedroom, he found that she had put fresh sheets on the mattress and had left him clean towels on the dresser. Now he lay there wondering what he'd gotten himself into and how he was going to get himself out of it.

Reflecting back on the day, something didn't feel right. Something was off, and he couldn't quite put his finger on it. Brennan lifted his arms above his head and clasped his hands together. He thought back to his conversations with Mr. and Mrs. Henley. And then he reflected on his questioning of Tobias Humphrey and his assistant Pamela. He thought back to everything he'd heard at the memorial service, the hushed whispers and choice words people didn't think anyone would hear or remember. He replayed each conversation over in his head. And it was on the third replay that what was bothering him clicked, the pieces falling into place.

Pamela had said that Rockwell's mother claimed Stella had made threats against her son. Mrs. Henley had told him the same thing. From what he'd been made to understand, Mrs. Henley had relayed her concerns to Tobias. But Tobias had clearly stated there had been no threats from Stella that he'd been aware of. None that had required his attention or police intervention. Now Brennan had to consider what had been the truth and who had been less than honest with him.

* * *

When Stella opened her eyes, the clock on her
nightstand read 2:15 a.m. She lay curled in a fetal
position in her bed, still in the dress she'd worn to
the memorial service. It had been a long day and she
was still feeling out of sorts. Thinking about what
had happened at Pratt Mansion left her shaking and
sent her into a fit of tears. She felt emotionally bat-
tered, slightly lost and monumentally embarrassed.

She appreciated Brennan's kindness. He had made
her feel safe and protected and not at all as foolish
as she felt over everything that had happened. She
should have stayed at home like he'd insisted. If she
had, then she wouldn't be feeling as vulnerable as
she was.

Hiding out in her bedroom had been necessary
for her to regroup and get herself together. She'd
needed time to herself. Time that hadn't required
her to explain herself or share her feelings. Time to
actually mourn the loss of someone she had cared
about. Time to process the wealth of emotion that felt
all-consuming. Time to revel in her own pity party
until she felt normal again.

She'd left Brennan to his own devices. She had
heard him puttering around in her kitchen, then he
had turned on the television, an episode of the old
television series *The Unit* playing loudly from her
family room. Just before she'd dozed off to sleep,
she'd heard him climb the steps, pausing in the hallway. She'd stood on her side of the entrance listening as she pondered whether or not to open the door

and invite him inside. The moment passed when she heard the guest room door close shut.

She'd questioned what she'd been thinking, then had laid back down, drawing her knees to her chest and wrapping her arms tightly around her body. Sleep had come on the tail end of one last good cry, the tears dampening her pillow. As slumber eased into her space, the sweetest inhale of air pulling at her gently, she heard Brennan's voice in her head, and Brennan was calling her *baby*.

It was a sweet memory, Stella thought as she rolled across the mattress. She threw her legs off the side and sat upright. Rising, she stripped out of her clothes and headed toward the shower. Hot water would feel good, she thought. The rest would fix itself in the morning. Because in the morning, Brennan would still be there trying to help her make sense of it all.

Brennan's phone rang, pulling him from a deep sleep. He didn't bother to open his eyes to check the caller ID before pulling it to his ear and depressing the answer button.

"Hello?"

"You alone?" Rory asked, her voice ringing loudly in his ear.

"And you're asking me that, why?"

"Because I saw how you were looking at Ms. Maxwell yesterday."

"Don't bust my balls, Rory. I'm not in the mood."

His cousin laughed. "How is she doing?"

"I don't know. She locked herself in her room

when we got back to her house, and I haven't seen her since."

"At least she's keeping her head down. That should make your job a whole lot easier."

"You think?"

Rory laughed. "Wishful thinking! I know how much you could use a break."

"What's up? You don't usually call so early in the morning."

"Just wanted to give you a heads-up. Wells needs you to give him an update on the Landmark Killer case."

"Something happen I need to know about?"

"He's got the mayor breathing down his neck. I informed the Henley family that we do not have a suspect in their son's murder, and now they're on a rampage. The mayor wants to make sure we don't give either case more priority than the other. Both are equally important for us to solve. But he needs both of them closed yesterday."

Brennan cursed. Logistically, it could take months for them to solve a murder case. Most especially when there was little to no evidence to point them in the right direction. The mayor's office poking around would only prove to be problematic. And unnecessary problems made for mistakes. "So, was that the bad news or the good news?" he asked.

"Who said anything about good news?" she countered.

"A man can hope, can't he?"

Rory laughed again. "Well, since I'm piling it on. There's a press conference this afternoon. The mayor wants Captain Reeves to give the public an update. It's supposed to calm nerves and ensure we stay transparent."

"So, tossing the bottom feeders a bone is supposed to keep them happy?"

"Calling the news media *bottom feeders* isn't cool. It's actually an insult to bottom feeders. Besides, I don't think your new friend will take kindly to you insulting her profession."

"You're right. I should be more creative with my choice of words. Do I need to be at this press conference?" Brennan asked.

"He'd like the whole team there, but we understand that you can't make it. We've got you covered."

"I owe you one," Brennan responded.

"Yes, you do."

Brennan sat upright, shifting his body to the side of the bed. "Things good otherwise?"

"Of course not, but that's a conversation for another day."

Brennan chuckled softly. "You know I've got your back, right, Rory?"

"Ditto. And please, keep that woman safe."

"Yes, ma'am, Detective Colton. I promise to return her just like you gave her to me."

As Rory disconnected the phone line, Brennan smiled, knowing his cousin was shaking her head at him.

The phone rang twice before Garrett Hoffman answered Stella's call.

"What's going on with you?" her friend questioned.

His voice was low and slightly muffled. Stella knew his hand was cupped over the receiver to keep nosy ears from hearing his conversation. "Girl, you made today's cover!"

"You're kidding me, right?"

"Of course! The boss shut that down, but there's a great shot of you going toe to toe with a Miss New York wannabe that's making the rounds here in the office. Did that heifer hit you?"

Stella rolled her eyes skyward. "You know good and well if that woman had put her hands on me, I would have made the front page mopping the floor with her."

"I know that's right. But really, what's going on?"

"First, why is Taylor calling me? She's left a dozen messages in my mailbox."

"She's trying to scoop an exclusive with you about the Henley killing. Your boss was ready to roll the story about you being arrested until they released you. Once your name was cleared, Taylor pitched doing a story on what happened and how journalists are falsely accused and weaponized when it's convenient for the status quo. Or some crap like that."

"I'm not giving her an exclusive. I'd write my own damn story if I thought it was newsworthy."

"Don't shoot me! I'm just sharing what I heard."

"What have they said about me taking a leave of absence?"

"Just that you needed some personal time until this all blows over. But someone from Human Resources came up to look through your desk yesterday."

"Damn vultures! My body's not even cold yet, and they're ready to give my desk away!"

"All I know is that there's some concern about your negative press reflecting badly on the newspaper. They just want it to die down before you come back."

"Yeah, right."

"It's what I heard."

Stella blew a soft sigh. "I need to get back to work, or I'm going to go crazy."

"Just take some time. You'll get past this. Stay in touch, and if I hear anything new, I promise I'll call you."

"Thank you, Garrett!"

"You're welcome, Stella! Keep the faith, girl!"

"I love you too, dude! I love you too!"

When Brennan finally made his way to the lower level of Stella's home, she was at the kitchen counter consuming a bowl of Frosted Flakes cereal. She looked like she had conquered the world and could have taken on another. Something like joy shone from her eyes and her complexion was crystal, not a single frown line to be found. He had worried what their first encounter might be like, but the sight of her eased every ounce of anxiety from his spirit.

"Good morning," he said, a wide smile filling his face.

Stella tossed up a hand. "Good morning! Did you sleep well?"

"Like a baby."

She pointed toward the Keurig machine on her

counter. "There's coffee and cereal if you're hungry. I'd cook, but I'm not in the mood."

"No problem. I would have gladly cooked for you."

"You've done that twice now. And I appreciate it. I'm sorry I missed last night's dinner."

"It'll be great for lunch. I put the leftovers in the refrigerator for you."

"Aren't you considerate?" she said.

Their conversation felt slightly awkward, almost mechanical, as if the ease they had previously felt had suddenly disappeared. Brennan sensed that Stella felt it as well.

"Look," he started to say, "I need to apologize…"

"I'm really sorry about yesterday…" Stella said at the same time.

They both paused and then laughed, and just like that, an air of comfort settled back over them.

Brennan took a seat on the stool beside her. "If I did anything yesterday to upset you or make you uncomfortable, I want to apologize. I would never want to overstep my boundaries with you."

"Not at all," Stella answered. "I'm the one who owes you an apology. I should have listened and kept my happy ass right here at home. I would never have purposely caused that kind of drama."

"I was concerned about your safety. I haven't forgotten that someone tried to come after you. For all we know, that someone was in the room yesterday."

Stella shook her head. "I wasn't thinking. What I did was reckless."

Brennan gave her another smile and nodded in

agreement. "It was reckless, but I understand it. You were grieving somebody you had loved once. You should have been allowed to do that without being harassed."

There was a moment of pause as the two considered each other. Brennan leaned across her countertop with a large mug of hot coffee pressed between his palms. Stella pulled a spoonful of cereal into her mouth.

"I think it's going to be eggs and bacon for me," Brennan said. "Can I interest you in a plate?"

Stella laughed, "What, you don't like cereal?"

He laughed with her. "I need a hearty meal. There is nothing hearty about cereal. Most especially sugar-coated corn flakes."

"What about all the athletes on the Wheaties boxes?"

"You're not eating Wheaties!"

Stella winced. "They're not my favorite, but if you need a heartier brand of cereal, I'll make sure there's always a box on hand just for you."

"Have I earned special privileges?" Brennan questioned, his brow raised.

Stella's gaze narrowed ever so slightly. "Don't get ahead of yourself, Special Agent Colton. *Special* is not that kind of special!"

The duo laughed heartily.

Stella sat and watched as Brennan prepared himself two eggs over easy with two slices of bacon and a single slice of buttered toast. She liked having him in her space, enjoying the camaraderie between them. She appreciated that he didn't take himself too seriously and that he made her laugh. With everything that had happened, she needed to laugh.

When he sat down to enjoy his morning meal, she rose from her seat to wash away the few dirty dishes that had piled up in her sink. She was growing comfortable with his presence, and although she didn't say anything, she wasn't sure how she felt about that. Most especially since Brennan Colton seemed very content to be sharing space and time with her.

"So, what's on your agenda today?" she asked.

"I'm going to have to leave you for a bit," Brennan said. "The mayor is planning a press conference this afternoon about the Landmark Killer case, and I need to meet with the team before that happens. I also want to follow up with Rockwell's business colleagues to see if any of them know anything."

"Did you find out anything yesterday?"

"Just what you already know. Everyone loved Rockwell, he was God's gift to us all and you should be our one and only suspect."

Stella winced. "Rockwell wasn't the prize people thought he was. Just ask Pamela."

Brennan's eyes widened. "Pamela? What about her?"

"Rockwell and Pamela were friends in school. Someone had set them up on a blind date. He showed up, ate his meal and then ducked out when the check came. She papered the entire campus with Photoshopped flyers of him in a dress or something crazy like that. He begged her for a second chance, made reservations at some five-star restaurant, then wined and dined her the entire weekend to make amends. They used to laugh about it, but I could tell that him being mean to her had hurt her feelings. She got even though, and obviously, they got past it. In fact, she was the one who recommended him to Tobias. I don't know if he would have even considered politics if she hadn't pushed him to run for office."

Brennan nodded. "Was Pamela close to Rockwell's mother?"

"Define close," Stella responded. "Silvia isn't your typical warm and fuzzy, cookie-baking PTA mom."

"Did they get along? Were they friends?"

"Actually, they seemed to be quite close. But then, Pamela is friendly with everyone. She likes to be helpful, and Mrs. Henley enjoys bossing people around. She had that poor girl running all kinds of errands for her and Pamela never complained."

"Interesting…" Brennan muttered, reflecting back on what he'd been thinking earlier.

"Not really," Stella said. "That whole little clique of theirs, including Tobias, made me itch!"

"What do you mean?"

"It was like some unholy alliance. They were always plotting together and covering for each other. It drove Rockwell crazy because he thought his mother was behind it."

"Did you agree?"

"No, I put my money on Tobias. He loved having Mrs. Henley's attention."

"Enough to be jealous of Rockwell?"

Stella paused, wiping her damp hands against a

dish towel. "I never really thought about it," she said finally. "He and Rockwell got along well. I never got jealousy vibes from Tobias."

"And nothing sketchy from Pamela?"

"I once thought she might have had a crush on Rockwell, but the way she chases after Tobias, I think she might be in love with him."

"And Tobias?"

"Tobias loves Tobias, like Silvia loves Silvia!"

"Do you think it's possible one of them killed Rockwell?"

Stella took her dear sweet time before she answered, giving the suggestion some serious thought. She finally shook her head. "No. I wouldn't think so. They were head of his fan club. They wanted him to do well. Obviously, anything is possible, but I don't see that."

Brennan nodded, moving to the sink to wash his plate and silverware.

"Why all the questions?" Stella asked. "What do you know?"

"Nothing. I'm just trying to cover all my bases."

"Want to know what's on my agenda today?"

"Does it involve showing up someplace you don't need to be?"

"Ha ha!" Stella said sarcastically. "It doesn't. In fact, I have no plans to leave the house. I plan to park myself on that sofa and binge-watch episodes of *Housewives of New York* while I stuff myself with chocolate chip cookies."

"You don't mean that bag of mini cookies that were in the cupboard, do you?"

Stella cut an eye in his direction, her tone suddenly changing. "Did you eat my cookies?"

"I might have had one or two or the entire bag last night."

She tossed up her hands, feigning frustration as she glared in his direction. "You don't want me to leave the house, but you eat all my snacks."

"I didn't eat them all."

"But you ate the best ones."

"I'll bring some cookies when I come back."

"You better." Stella pushed her bottom lip out in a pretend pout.

Brennan laughed. "There will be a patrol car outside keeping an eye on things while I'm gone. Courtesy of my cousin Rory. Please stay out of trouble while I'm gone, Stella."

The look Stella gave him was priceless. There were daggers shooting from her eyes, and she was biting back a retort that probably would have cut him deep. With a nod of his head, Brennan hurried to the front door. He waved good-bye as he made his exit.

"I won't be long," he called over his shoulder.

As the door closed and locked behind him, Stella grinned, thinking she couldn't wait for him to return.

Chapter 9

The internet is forever. Stella remembered the first time she'd heard the statement, thinking *forever* was only as long as the systems that held it in place. Eventually, all things came to an end. Now, scrolling through the numerous photos, stories and opinions of her encounter with the Henley family and the conspiracy theories on how she was connected to Rockwell's murder, *forever* felt like an unending attack that she would never be able to recover from. She should have kept watching the *Housewives*, she thought. Even that absurdity didn't feel quite so painful. She heaved a deep sigh, closing the lid to her laptop.

For a split second, she wanted to cry. Then she didn't. Raging would have made her feel better. But she didn't have the energy for that either. She stole a look at her cell phone. She thought about calling Brennan but figured that wouldn't be a great idea. They weren't friends like that, and there was nothing wrong that she needed to report. But they were friends like that, she thought, suddenly questioning her relationship with the handsome man. *Weren't they?*

She decided to text him a message instead. She sat in thought as she pondered what to say. With a quick push of the buttons, she typed, deleted, typed then typed some more until she was happy with the message. She paused one last time and then she hit Send.

A noise at her front door suddenly pulled at her attention. She moved to the window to peek out. A postal delivery truck had pulled up out front, and the delivery person was standing in conversation with the police officer. The two men were chatting easily.

Moving to the front door, Stella pulled it open, looking from one to the other. She lifted her hand in greeting. "Hi, Pete!"

"Hi, Stella! I have a package for you. Online shopping again?"

Stella laughed. Most of her shopping was online, so she and the delivery persons for the neighborhood had become well acquainted. So much so that they were on a first name basis with each other, shared stories about work and family, and every Christmas, she gave the regulars a gift card.

The police officer chimed in. "My wife is just as bad. She's taken to hiding the boxes before I get home, hoping I don't see them!"

"That's why I don't need a husband." Stella laughed, the two men joining her.

"It's from someplace called the Rose Wheel?" the officer questioned. "Something you're expecting?"

Stella shrugged. "I buy from them regularly. I don't remember ordering anything recently, but that doesn't mean it isn't mine."

The officer laughed again as he took the midsize box from the man named Pete.

What came next would always be a blur in Stella's mind. She would remember the police officer starting up the short length of brick steps, that box extended out in front of him. She had taken a single step down, intent on meeting him halfway. Before she could take that second step, the entire world exploded before her eyes. Neither Pete nor the police officer were standing in front of her, and what remained of that box was nothing but dust blowing off into the distance. The sound of the explosion resonated from one corner of the block to the other. The force of it was so intense that Stella felt her entire body being lifted off her feet as she was thrown backward, slamming hard against her front door. As she fell to the concrete landing of her front steps, she heard herself cry out. Her voice sounded muffled with pain and confusion. Tears ran over her checks, and her head felt heavy against her thin neck. There was a ringing in her ears and a sharp pain vibrating through her head.

She lay perfectly still for as long as she could. Her eyes were closed, and time seemed to spin in slow motion. At the sound of sirens, Stella forced herself to open her eyes, wanting to see the cavalry when they arrived. She imagined that they would ride in like soldiers on white horses, determined to save the day. The sun was still shining brightly, but dark wisps of smoke trailed upward, marring the beauty of a crisp blue sky.

Stella heard voices, a cacophony of noise that didn't make any sense. She felt cold and her body began to shake. She wanted to lift her hand and wipe her eyes, but her arm was too heavy, and she was too tired. She closed her eyes again and waited. Brennan would be home soon, she thought. Brennan would wipe away her tears. Brennan would bring home those cookies.

Brennan hadn't planned to be in his office for as long as he had. He'd been trying to leave for the past hour, but the phone wouldn't stop ringing and agents wouldn't stop asking him questions. He finally pushed himself from his desk, hanging up the phone with the intention of leaving when Xander Washer poked his head through the door.

"Sorry to be a bother, but do you have a minute?" Xander questioned. Xander was the assistant to the FBI director, Roberta Chang. He knew Brennan would give him however many minutes he needed.

"How's it going, Xander?" Brennan responded. "What can I do for you?"

"Director Chang is stuck at an agency meeting in Washington. I have to send her an update on everyone's case load, and I hear you pulled a side job with the local police department investigating a murder?"

Brennan nodded. "The 130th precinct caught the murder of a local political candidate. We initially thought it might be related to the Landmark Killer case, but thus far, I haven't found any connection."

"Can you get me something in writing by tomorrow morning? I spoke with Detective Colton, and she said her office requested you. That you had ties to the case that they thought would be useful. She says you knew the suspect, who's now a potential victim?"

Brennan struggled not to laugh out loud. He'd have to thank Rory later, he thought. He nodded. "Yes," he said. "It's a complicated case. But I did clear it with Sergeant Blackthorn of the NYPD. I didn't want there to be any conflicts with our two offices."

"I'm sure Director Chang will appreciate that!" Xander said. "Just get me a brief update on everything you're working on. It'll be a big help."

"No problem," Brennan responded. "How's everything going with you?"

"No complaints. The job is keeping me busy. In a good way."

"Well, if there is anything I can give you a hand with, don't hesitate to ask."

Xander smiled and gave him a slight salute. "Let's grab a beer sometime. I don't get out much."

Brennan chuckled. "Say no more. I know what that's like. Just let me know when. I'll be there."

The young man nodded and disappeared down the hallway. Although he'd been with the agency for some time, Brennan hadn't had an opportunity to get to know him well. He was quiet, staying to himself most of the time. But he was popular with the women in the agency, his GQ looks garnering him much attention. Director Chang often remarked how fortunate she'd been to hire him.

Brennan made a mental note to document his cases as requested. He was ready to make his exit when his cell phone chimed for his attention. He paused to read the message on the screen, realizing he'd missed an incoming text message. He smiled as he read it quickly.

I'm missing my chocolate chip cookies.

The device chimed a second time, signaling an incoming call. He eyed the caller ID and answered it on the third ring. "Rory! I was just about to call you!" he said, his good mood vibrating through the telephone line.

"There's been an incident," Rory said, her tone tempered. "They've taken Stella to Mount Sinai Hospital. I need you to meet me there."

"What's happened?" Brennan said, hurrying out the door as they spoke.

"There was a bomb," Rory replied, and then she disconnected the call.

Brennan's good mood was suddenly shattered.

Stella hadn't spoken much since waking up in the hospital. Between local police, agents from Homeland Security and the FBI, she had answered more than her fair share of questions. She didn't have much else to share with anyone.

This time she'd made the front page of every major newspaper in the city. Peter Vincente, an employee of Federal Parcel Service and Officer Alfonzo Barrett, a ten-year veteran of the New York Police Department were both memorialized in the columns beside the story of the bombing. Both were survived by wives and children, and every time Stella thought about it, she withdrew into herself, nothing at all to say to anyone.

Online, photos of her home and the ensuing damage from the bomb blast scrolled in rotation with those earlier images from Rockwell's memorial. Someone had even gotten pictures of her sprawled out at the top of her steps and of her being taken away on a stretcher. But none of that mattered anymore. All Stella could think about was that someone had tried to kill her and took two innocent persons instead.

It had been a whole week since her world had been upended yet again, and all Stella wanted was to go home.

She looked up as Brennan gathered her belongings. There was an overnight bag with a change of clothing that he had packed for her and a multitude of floral arrangements sent to wish her well. One even included a cellophane balloon that read, Get Well Soon.

"I'm going to take these to the car," Brennan said softly. "The nurse should be here soon with the wheelchair to bring you down. I'll be right out front waiting for you. Okay?"

Stella nodded as he reached for her hand and squeezed her fingers. She wanted to smile, but every muscle in her body still hurt. She was badly bruised, looking like she'd gone ten rounds with a heavy-weight boxer. She also had stitches, twenty-three total, that closed gashes across her shoulder and the back of her head. She'd had a concussion, and it only when they were certain the head injury would not be permanent did the doctors agree to let her convalesce in her own bed.

Brennan hadn't left her side since he'd arrived at the hospital. He proclaimed himself her next of kin, ensuring that she'd had the best care. She had no idea when he'd found time to sleep or work, because every time she opened her eyes, he was there watching over her. He had been the only one who hadn't asked her any questions.

The drive back to her home was a quiet ride. Brennan's radio played oldies from the seventies and eighties. Simon and Garfunkel's "Bridge over Troubled Water" played softly out of the speakers. Stella was surprised that she remembered the words, and she hummed along with the tune as Brennan made the trek across the borough.

As he turned onto her block, she braced herself, certain the emotion that would come might be over-whelming. She was not prepared for the new railing and replacement bricks and concrete that had returned the front of her home to almost new. No hint of the blast remained. Her head snapped in Brennan's direction.

"You did this?"

He shook his head. "No. I didn't. The Henleys made all of this happen. Mr. Henley said they felt bad about everything that had occurred and were concerned knowing whoever killed their son might be trying to kill you too. He said he and his wife were also grateful that someone who cared about their son was there when he took his last breath."

"Wow!" Stella said. "Just wow!"

Minutes later, she was settled comfortably on her living room sofa. Brennan wanted her in bed, but she refused. She'd had enough of lying around. She was ready for a semblance of normalcy, if such a thing were possible.

Brennan had made himself comfortable in her kitchen, promising a meal that would rival everything she had ever eaten in the past. He was trying to take her mind off the memories, wanting her to find a level of comfort in the space that had been violated by someone else's obsession with her. She followed him into the room and took a seat at the counter.

"You're supposed to be resting," he said. He shook a metal spatula in her direction.

"I thought I'd pour myself a glass of wine."

"You know you can't mix alcohol with the pain meds you're on. Not going to happen on my watch."

"Who deemed you my keeper?"

"You did. You were whispering my name when they took you to the hospital. I was called and I came. Now you're going to have a hard time getting rid of me."

Stella smiled. "Well, it's a good thing I like having you around," she said. "Good friends are hard to come by."

She gave him a quick glance, waiting for a reaction, but there was none. At least, not what she'd expected. He glanced back and amusement danced in his eyes.

"Dinner's going to be a minute," he said. "Do you want a snack?"

"I'm going to need something! The hospital food was horrible. I'll probably have nightmares over it."

Brennan moved to her pantry and swung open the door. "I think I have something for that," he said. He pointed inside and Stella shifted her gaze to see what he found so amusing. Inside, an entire shelf had been dedicated to her favorite bag of chocolate chip cookies.

"I would only do this for my friends," he said, his tone smug.

Stella laughed. The first good laugh she'd had in a long while.

Brennan poked his head into Stella's bedroom to check on how she was doing. She'd fallen asleep shortly after dinner and was still snoring softly beneath the large down comforter that adorned her bed. It had been a few rough days for her, and she had been desperate for those things that were familiar to her.

Much had happened while she'd been in the hospital. Brennan had interviewed more people, followed up on other leads and was still no closer to solving her case or finding the Landmark Killer. With the bombing, additional manpower was now helping with the investigation, and they still hadn't gotten anywhere.

He had been worried that she wouldn't want to

return to her family's home. What happened would be hard for anyone to overcome, but Stella had been adamant that the Harlem brownstone would be the best medicine she would ever need.

He left her bedroom door ajar in case she wakened and called for him. He eased back down the stairs and settled himself against the living room sofa. He debated whether or not to turn on the television but decided against it. He needed to think, and for the first time since Rory had called with the bad news, his head was clear enough for him to focus.

He revisited the details of Rockwell's murder and the conversations he'd had with everyone he'd spoken with. Nothing made sense, and he was starting to feel as if he were spinning his wheels and going nowhere fast. He needed help and he didn't have a problem asking for it. Reaching for his cell phone on the table, he sent a text message to his cousin Sinead. Minutes later, her response vibrated on the telephone screen. She promised to meet him the next day.

With a deep sigh, Brennan sent one last text message to the patrolmen watching the home outside. He stood and moved to the window, lifting the blinds so that they could see him. He checked the door lock and shut off the lights. Sitting back down, he leaned his head back and blew another deep breath out of his lungs. He was exhausted, and ready to close his eyes. Stella was home and safe. He looked forward to a good night's sleep. He had a long day ahead of him, and he needed to be ready for whatever might come his way.

Chapter 10

Brennan had grabbed a table in the Starbucks on Madison Avenue. His cousin Sinead had chosen the location. Arriving before she did, he ordered a hot coffee for himself and her favorite chai tea latte with steamed soy milk. When she came through the doors, he lifted the familiar green-and-white cup and waved it at her.

Sinead waved back, greeted him with a nod and one of the brightest smiles he'd seen in a very long time. She moved to the table and took the seat beside him, leaning to kiss his cheek as she sat down. In line with most agents in the FBI, she rarely took a seat with her back to the door.

Sinead exuded confidence and strength and the attitude that she was ready to fight tooth and nail for everything she believed in. She was one of the best FBI profilers in the field and rarely missed the small details that helped them solve their cases.

"What's up, cousin!" she chimed, grabbing the coffee cup from him and taking a sip.

"You tell me," he answered. "I need help!"

Sinead nodded. "I heard things have been rough."

"I'm spinning my wheels and getting absolutely nowhere."

"How's Ms. Maxwell?"

Brennan's brow lifted and he shrugged. "She's struggling. She doesn't want anyone to know, but I can see it. Someone tried to kill her. They almost did, and two people died in the process. That's a tough pill for anyone to swallow."

Sinead took another sip of her morning brew.

"Did you get a chance to review the materials I sent you?"

She nodded. "I did. I also saw the video of the murder." She sat back in her seat. "Everyone's assumed the murder was all about the victim. But so far, you haven't been able to find a motive that makes any sense. You do know someone went to a lot of trouble to make sure Stella showed up when the victim died. So, let's consider this has everything to do with Stella and Stella, alone. Someone wanted her in that alley, and they made certain to get her there for whatever reason. Right after, someone tries to grab her and that fails. Then, a day later, a bomb is mailed to her home. Everything thus far says this is all about Stella Maxwell."

"That had already crossed my mind, but I hit a wall

there as well. Stella hasn't allowed too many people into her personal space."

"Well, whoever it is, you can bet they're going to come for her again. You and she both need to be ready. You also need to consider that maybe, your perp is female, with a grudge. Because in all honesty, this feels like jealousy energy. Is there someone who didn't want her to be in a relationship with the boyfriend? Or someone she pissed off in her line of work? You may need to dig a little deeper into her past to find the answers."

"Really? You really think the perp is female?"

"Statistically, although the percentage of women who offend is low, women are more inclined to be emotionally invested in the persons they kill."

"But the victim was Rockwell, not Stella!"

"Is it possible Stella was the intended victim, and Rockwell was supposed to find her body? That who-ever called her did so knowing she would show up if for no other reason than to get a story? Maybe Rockwell arrived early and threw off their plans? Which is why they keep coming for her. Trying to finish the job."

Brennan's eyes danced from side to side as he pon-dered his cousin's comment. Everything she'd said made sense, but then it didn't, opening a whole other can of worms that had him baffled. Because if Stella had been the intended victim, then who was gunning for her and why?

"What about the video?" Brennan questioned. "Nothing stood out?"

"Nothing that hinted at the identity of your perp. The body frame was slight, which could definitely indicate the killer was female, but it could also be a man with a small body frame. The victim wasn't an overly big guy either."

Thoughts of Tobias shot through Brennan's mind. Tobias fit the physical description, but he lacked motive. He had nothing to gain from Rockwell's death. And nothing against Stella that Brennan was aware of.

For the next hour, the two tossed possible scenarios back and forth at each other. Brennan realized he would need to revisit the women he had previously interviewed. And any other woman connected to Rockwell and Stella that he might not have considered. Maybe Silvia Henley wasn't the doting mother and had more involvement than Brennan gave her credit for. He hadn't met any of Stella's friends, but maybe it was time he did so. Maybe someone calling themselves her friend really wasn't.

"I can't afford for this case to go cold," Brennan said.

Sinead nodded her understanding. "I get it, so start thinking outside of the box."

Brennan shifted the conversation. "Anything new on the Landmark Killer case? No new messages?"

"Not a thing," Sinead responded. "He's gone quiet. The team is still beating the pavement down in the theater district, but no one's coming up with anything."

"I hate my job," Brennan muttered, pulling both hands over his face.

Sinead laughed. "And that would be a lie."

"Yeah, maybe, but there are days."

"So, what's going on with you and this woman? I hear you two have gotten very friendly and that you're still staying at her home?"

"Where'd you hear that?"

Sinead grinned as she shrugged her shoulders. "A little birdie told me."

"You must be talking to Rory."

"You know better than anyone that my sister and I don't share like that."

"I thought things had gotten better with you two?"

"They have, but we still have issues."

"So, who said something?" Brennan leaned forward, folding his hands together atop the table. "I need to know who's talking before they get me in trouble with my director, your boyfriend, and lose me my job."

"*Your* twin likes to talk!" Sinead finally said. "And I don't think you'll have a problem with the bosses. Wells and I are a thing now, after all. Unless Stella really is guilty and you try to cover for her."

Brennan laughed. "I'm going to kill Cash!"

"If you do, I'll try to make sure you and Ms. Maxwell get side-by-side jail cells," Sinead said with a hearty laugh.

After waving good-bye to Sinead, Brennan debated where to go next. He was still mulling over the prospect of the perpetrator being female. Not that he didn't know women could kill, but he was having a hard time pinpointing a potential suspect who was laser-focused on taking down Stella. Who despised her that much and why?

Two telephone calls later, and he was headed back to the former campaign offices for Rockwell Henley. Tobias had agreed to meet him there. Brennan had no doubt the man was more than curious to learn what Brennan knew, not that Brennan would be eyeing him sideways for the crime. Pamela and Tobias had alibied each other, both claiming to have been at campaign headquarters when Rockwell had been murdered. Brennan couldn't help but wonder if the two could possibly be covering for each other. He might be wrong, he thought, but he couldn't afford to not question every single lead in front of him.

When Brennan reached campaign headquarters, he was surprised to discover Henley had been replaced. The office was open, staffed and promoting a brand-new candidate. A man named Marshall Tucker. Posters with Marshall Tucker's image had been hung in the windows and all around the space.

As Brennan stood looking around, actually surprised by the swift transition, Tobias came rushing from the back, seeming eager to have Brennan there. The two men shook hands.

"I appreciate you taking time to talk to me," Brennan said casually.

"Not a problem. The team is stuffing envelopes today and cold-calling perspective campaign donors. I've just been catching up on some paperwork, so I appreciate being able to take a break." He turned and gestured for Brennan to follow.

They headed toward the back of the building, Tobias leading him down a short hallway to an office in the rear. The space was quiet, and when Tobias closed the door, any noise coming from the front was nonexistent. He pointed Brennan to a cushioned chair as he eased behind the desk.

"Marshall Tucker?" Brennan said, pointing at the poster behind Tobias's head.

The other man shrugged. "He was the party's second choice. Since the deadline to run hadn't passed, they decided to throw him into the ring." He leaned forward across the desk, the gesture feeling conspiratorial. "Between me and you, Rockwell was a better choice, but we have to work with what we have. Unfortunately, Marshall's penchant for too much wine and too many women will eventually be his downfall."

"So, why support him?"

"We need that seat. As long as he sticks to script and does what he's told, we're willing to help him get the crown."

"And that's why politics and politicians get a bad rap," Brennan said.

Tobias laughed. "Since I know you didn't come here to debate the political climate with me, tell me how I can help you."

"I want to talk about Stella," Brennan said.

"I thought she'd been cleared of any wrongdoing?"

"She has. But Rockwell's killer is still targeting her, and I need to figure out why."

"I don't know that I can help you with that."

"Knowing how deeply the party vets everyone associated with your candidates, I know that if there was something to find out about Ms. Maxwell, you've found it."

"I wish I could hand you a file that's six inches thick. But in all honesty, working for that rag newspaper was her biggest crime."

"I'm told you weren't a fan of Stella's."

"I wouldn't say that. My job, Agent Colton, is to get the party's candidate elected to office. Part of that process is building an image that voters want to get behind and support. Stella didn't fit into the image we wanted for Mr. Henley."

"And what image was that?"

"Their relationship was too…well…" Tobias hesitated, seeming to strain his mind for the right words. Or not to say the wrong thing. Finally, he said, "In a nutshell, it was just too liberal. The party wanted to showcase his conservative edge. They wanted him to emulate the family values his parents projected."

"And their relationship didn't fit that image?"

"Stella wouldn't play her part. She refused to be dutiful and obedient."

"Was Rockwell seeing anyone else?"

"Define seeing?"

"Did he have other women, or another woman he was involved with?" Brennan chuckled.

It was at that moment that Pamela poked her head into the room. "Tobias, we need—" she suddenly paused, seeing Brennan for the first time "—Agent Colton! What a surprise!" she gushed.

"Miss Littlefield…"

"Can it wait, Pamela?" Tobias interjected.

"Of course," she responded, that bright smile filling her face. "It's good to see you again, Agent," she said as she stepped back out of the room and closed the door.

As Brennan turned his attention back to Tobias, the man was rolling his eyes skyward. Realizing that Brennan had caught him, he tried to explain himself.

"Pamela is a wonderful employee, but she can be a little too helpful sometimes. Now, to go back to your question—no, Rockwell had great integrity. He was totally committed to whoever he was dating. He truly had feelings for Stella, but she wasn't a great fit."

"Because…?"

"Because she was too strong-willed and refused to stay in her place. Stella's aspirations went against the grain of the image we had for Rockwell. He agreed."

He was a bigger jerk than I initially thought he was, Brennan thought. He didn't say so out loud, but he had no doubt that Tobias could read the emotion on his face.

"Did he and Pamela ever date?" Brennan asked.

"Pamela? Oh, no! They were just friends. Pamela has a boyfriend she's been with since elementary school. His name's Tyson something or other. He's a little challenged from what I understand. Social situations bother him, so he rarely leaves their home. She's totally dedicated to him."

Tobias's phone rang, and he reached for the device

on his desk. "I need to get back to work, so if you don't have any other questions, Agent Colton…"

"Thanks for your time," Brennan answered as he turned toward the door.

Tobias's voice rang out as Brennan made his exit. "Marshall Tucker for Governor! How may I help you?"

Brennan was three blocks away when he stopped to place a call. It rang twice in his ear before it was answered, the voice on the other end surprising him.

"Agent Colton's office. This is Xander, how may I help you?"

"Xander, hey, it's Brennan. I was trying to reach Cash. I'm surprised to hear your voice."

"Brennan, hello! I was just leaving some files on your brother's desk when the phone rang. I knew it might be important, so I answered it. We try to be efficient around here."

Brennan chuckled. "No problem, dude. We all appreciate what you do. Is he around?"

"He's out in the field. Is there anything I can help you with?"

"Just leave a message for him, please. I need him to run a full background check for me. The party's name is Pamela Littlefield."

"Is this related to the Landmark Killer case?" Xander asked.

"No, she's a potential suspect in the Rockwell Henley murder and the assault on Stella Maxwell."

Brennan could hear the man scribbling notes on paper. "Got it," Xander said.

"Thank you. I appreciate your help. And just tell Cash to call me when he has a chance."

"Will do. Be safe out there, Agent," Xander said before disconnecting the call.

Appreciating the sentiment, Brennan nodded into the receiver as if Xander could see him. Minutes later, he was headed back to Harlem.

When Brennan finally arrived back at the Maxwell home, Stella was out in the backyard. She was sitting on the patio sunning herself. A copy of the most recent *New Yorker* magazine lay across her lap. She'd lit the gas grill, and billows of smoke were seeping out the sides. Whatever was roasting beneath the lid scented the air.

"You're cooking?" he said as he moved to the lawn chair beside her.

"Hello to you too! And yes, I'm cooking. I'm smoking a pork shoulder for dinner. It should be done in another hour or so."

"It smells good."

"It does, doesn't it?"

Brennan smiled. He'd missed her. He'd been worried about her. But he didn't say so. He hoped she would know without him telling her. Because he didn't have the words to say what he wanted. Nor could he, given the circumstances of their situation.

"I had a good day," Stella said, as if reading his mind. "How about you?"

"Not as productive as I would have liked, but then some days are like that."

"Aren't you tired of babysitting me?" Stella said. "I imagine you'd probably like to go back to your own home and life by now."

"My job is my life, and I'm perfectly fine right now. Making sure you're safe is a priority for me."

"Well, I'm glad I give your life some purpose," she said teasingly.

Brennan laughed. "Anything I can do to help with dinner?"

Stella shook her head. "Just stay out of my kitchen so I can show you how real professionals do it."

With a nod of his head, Brennan stood back up. "In that case, I'm going upstairs to take a shower and change."

"I hung your clothes in the guest room closet," Stella said. "And I did your laundry. If you plan to stay, there's no reason for you to live out of your suitcase."

His eyes widened. "Thank you. I didn't intend for you to—" he started to say.

Stella interrupted him. "Don't make a big deal out of it. I just know the sacrifices you're making to be here. I just wanted to show you my appreciation."

Brennan dropped his hand to her shoulder and gave it a light squeeze. Moving back into the home, he didn't have anything else to say.

Dinner was divine! As Brennan filled his plate for the third time, Stella had to praise her own cooking. As her late father use to say, she put her foot in that meal. The meat was perfection, tender enough to cut with a plastic fork and melting like butter in your mouth.

She'd sliced it thin and served it with baked macaroni and cheese and turnip greens. It was a Sunday-after-church meal, the likes of which reminded her of her family's Southern roots. It was comfort food from the first bite to the last.

Brennan hummed his appreciation. "If I eat another bite, I'm going to burst," he said. "This is so good!"

"Thank you. Save some room for dessert though. I made banana pudding."

"I don't think I've ever had banana pudding," he said. "Well, maybe I have. The kind that comes in a box."

"This is homemade. With vanilla wafer cookies. There's no box involved in my banana pudding."

For the first time that day, Brennan was relaxed, and Stella could see it on his face. He had showered and changed into sweatpants and a T-shirt. The casual attire fit his personality, and she liked that he had made himself comfortable in her home.

She changed the subject as she lifted the empty dinner plates from the table. "The Henleys called me today. Well, Mr. Henley called me."

"What did he say?"

"He just wanted to check that I was doing well. They'd gotten my thank-you note for the work they did on the house."

"Mrs. Henley still hasn't warmed up?"

"She said hello. That's about as warm as she'll ever get."

"They're both giving the mayor hell about the investigation. They think other cases are taking precedence over finding their son's killer. They're breathing down her neck, she's breathing down the FBI director's neck and the director is breathing down my neck."

Brennan had risen from his own seat to help Stella with the dirty dishes. She washed and he dried, the duo standing side by side at her kitchen sink.

Stella nodded. "You can understand their frustration. I want the case closed too. And I know exactly what you're going through trying to find his killer."

"And keep you safe from this monster," Brennan added.

Stella smiled. Quiet descended over the room, and each fell into their own thoughts. When the dishes were washed and put away, she pointed him to the family room. "*Family Feud* is about to start. Turn up the television while I get us some dessert."

Brennan shook his head. "Really, Stella? *Family Feud*?"

"Don't criticize. Just turn on the TV, please. I like Steve Harvey."

"You and every other woman."

"That's not true. Some women don't appreciate Steve's relationship advice."

"Why?"

"Because a man who's been married and divorced multiple times isn't the relationship guru he'd like people to believe he is."

"Tell me more."

"Nope, I just want to watch mindless TV and relax. If we start talking relationships, you'll probably get your feelings hurt, and then I'll have to deal with your emotional fallout."

"My emotional fallout?"

"You men can be especially sensitive when we say things you don't like."

Brennan laughed and Stella laughed with him.

Minutes later the two were sitting side by side on the sofa, bowls of warm banana pudding in their laps. Brennan hummed with each spoonful into his mouth, and Stella giggled at his enthusiasm.

"I think we should open a restaurant," Brennan said. "We'd make a fortune if you cooked like this."

"Why do I have to cook?" she asked.

"Because I could never recreate this and have it taste half as good."

"At least you know it," she replied. "But let's not share it with the world. It'll be our little piece of heaven here at home."

"I'm saying let's just share it with the five boroughs! We can take on the world next year!"

Stella grabbed his empty bowl and rose from her seat. "Do you want more?" she asked.

He shook his head. "Maybe later. I couldn't eat another bite right now."

Turning, Stella moved into the kitchen. She washed the dessert dishes and was wiping down the kitchen counter when Brennan's cell phone vibrated. He'd left the device there when he was drying the dishes and putting them back into the cupboards.

She called into the other room. "Your phone is beeping! Do you want me to bring it to you?"

"Yes, please!" he called back.

Picking up the device, Stella glanced down at the screen. An incoming text message was chiming for his attention. She carried the phone back to the family room, handed it to him and sat back down. She reached for a lightweight cotton throw that rested on the sofa arm and draped it over her legs. She watched as Brennan pushed buttons and then scrolled.

The change in his temperament flipped so quickly that it surprised her. Stella didn't expect his reaction as he suddenly shifted forward in his seat. His jaw tightened, the lines in his face hardening like stone. His eyes narrowed into thin slits, and for a split second, he looked like he was ready to spit venom.

"What's going on?" she asked, shifting her body closer to his. "What's wrong, Brennan?"

He shook his head but didn't speak. Rage seeped from his eyes.

"You're scaring me," Stella said, her voice dropping an octave.

Brennan passed her his phone, the two exchanging the briefest of looks. Putting the device into her hands, Stella read the message on the screen.

Shouldn't you be out looking for me, Agent Colton? Instead, you're shacking up with a murder suspect. I thought you Coltons didn't like killers since that one who got to your dear old daddy? I'm still out here, Agent. I'm headed to the theater. See you on Broadway!

"What's going on?" Stella said. "Who sent this to you?"

Brennan tossed her a look. He took a deep breath and then he answered.

"The Landmark Killer."

Chapter 11

It wasn't an hour later before Brennan's team was crowded into Stella's living room. She had brewed a large pot of coffee and plated the last bit of banana pudding. His cousin Sinead and the NYPD's lead investigator Wells Blackthorn had arrived first. Brennan's fraternal twin, Cash, arrived next, followed by his brother Patrick and Rory Colton. Ashlyn Colton arrived last, not at all happy to have been pulled from a date with a hedge fund manager. Waves of anxiety flooded the room, the wealth of it like an electrical current flowing from one to the other.

"This son of a bitch is playing games with us," Patrick Colton snarled.

Stella turned to stare at the man. He was angry, hostility spewing with every word. The family resemblance was strong, although his hair was browner than Brennan's, she thought. And she hadn't ever seen Brennan rage like that.

"He knows us," Brennan snapped. "He knows too much about us."

"Well, it's personal now," Rory said.

"It's been personal," Sinead replied, the two women glancing toward each other.

"Clearly, for him to know this much about all of you, he has access to your personal records," Wells said calmly. "One of our agencies has a mole."

"Or he's efficiently stalking us all," Ashlyn countered.

"It has to be someone we work with," Brennan said. "How would he know where I am if he wasn't with one of our offices?"

"So, you think they're NYPD?" Rory asked.

Brennan shook his head. "I didn't say that. It could easily be someone at the FBI's Manhattan office. We don't know, but we need to figure it out and figure it out fast."

"Who've you pissed off lately?" Patrick asked, lifting his brow as he tossed Brennan a look.

"You'd get a shorter list if you asked him who he hasn't pissed off," Cash interjected.

Nervous laughter filled the room. Stella took the opportunity to interrupt their conversation. "Can I get anything for anyone?" she asked.

All eyes were suddenly on her. She gave them the slightest smile. "There's no more banana pudding, but I've got cookies. Chocolate chip."

"Thank you," Sinead answered. "We're good. And that pudding was to die for. I'd ask for the recipe, but I know I won't make it."

"It was good," Ashlyn said. "And we apologize for the intrusion. It's nice to meet you though. Our big brother is quite smitten with you."

"Shut up, Ashlyn," Brennan said, his cheeks turning a deep shade of fire-engine read.

They all laughed.

"Well, it's my pleasure to meet all of you," Stella said.

Cash turned the conversation back to the topic at hand. "Whoever it is, him throwing our father into his sick games is going to get him hurt," he said, still seething.

Heads nodded in agreement.

Wells interjected again. "Let's toss out some names at both departments. People you're close with. Anyone you've had run-ins with. Let's see if we can narrow it down. And let's focus on Sinead and Brennan first, since they received the first two messages. Any other cases you two have in common? Anyone you two both worked with or had issues with?"

Like a fly on the wall, Stella sat back and listened as the family did what they did best. It was interesting to watch them analyze information and bounce ideas off each other. It also made her realize how much she missed her own work. How she would like to be on a case, doing the investigative work to tell a story no one knew. Finding the details that blew something wide open and shone a spotlight on something relevant. In that moment, she realized it was past time for her to get back to work. She made a mental note to call the senior editor the following morning to plead her case.

Sinead stole a glance at the clock on the wall. "Wells and I need to get home," she said, "before the sitter calls child services on us for abandoning our baby."

Wells laughed. "We haven't abandoned our baby. The sitter knows how this works."

"Well, I miss baby Harry, and I want to snuggle him one last time before he goes off to sleep."

"Isn't it past his bedtime?" Ashlyn questioned. "Babies go to sleep early, don't they?"

"She will wake him up to put him back to sleep," Wells said with a shake of his head.

Sinead laughed. "I am not that bad!"

"He's such a sweet baby," Rory said softly.

Wells leaned in to give Sinead's sister a hug. "You're welcome to come and visit him anytime," he said.

Sinead smiled. "Especially since we might need a new sitter if we don't get out of here."

Patrick waved his hand excitedly. "I volunteer!"

Brennan looked from one face to the other. "We're all going to be available if we don't get some answers soon."

Cash nodded. "I can't do diapers!" he said, wincing. "Diapers terrify me."

Laughter rang warmly as they all headed for the door at the same time. Ashlyn moved to Stella's side and hugged her warmly. "We're glad you're doing okay. You had us worried there for a while."

"Thank you."

"When this is all over, let's do lunch or something. Get to know each other better."

"I'd like that."

Ashlyn winked an eye at her and exited the home. Brennan watched as his family went their separate ways. When the street outside was quiet, he waved at the patrol car parked across the way. A plainclothes officer waved back. Brennan shut the door and secured the lock. When he turned back to the family room, Stella had already collected the dirty dishes and had tossed them into the dishwasher.

"You're using the dreaded dishwasher?" Brennan said, surprised that she wasn't handwashing them.

"We're both tired. And I still have questions," she said.

He gave her a look. "Questions?"

They moved back into the family room and sat down. Stella turned to face him, folding her legs beneath her as she sat cross-legged.

"I'd like to know more about your father and why the mention of him was so disconcerting for everyone."

Hesitancy crossed Brennan's face like a dark cloud billowing in front of him. His jaw tightened, and the light that had been shining in his eyes dimmed.

Realizing she'd hit a nerve, Stella reached out and touched his arm. Manicured fingers tapped lightly against the soft flesh. Concern washed over her expression. Concern for his well-being and curiosity lifted her gaze.

Brennan pulled himself from her touch. The gesture startled them both, and he saw a look of hurt seep from Stella's eyes. He grabbed her hand, contrition furrowing his brow. "I'm sorry. It just..." He heaved a deep sigh, emotion stealing the words from him. He apologized a second time. "I'm really sorry. I didn't pull away because of anything you did."

"It's okay," Stella said. She shifted her body back ever so slightly, putting a hint of distance between them. "I just wanted to understand."

He took another deep breath. "You have a right to know. I'm just surprised, though, that after all these years, it still hurts as much as it does." A gust of air eased past his thin lips as he continued. "My father was Mike Colton. Michael Patrick Colton. He was a dedicated police officer; a beat cop who proudly walked the streets in the Bronx. When we were kids, he was brutally murdered. By a serial killer. Ashlyn was still a baby at the time. She never even got to know him the way Cash, Patrick and I did."

Stella reached out and touched him again. "Brennan, I'm so sorry. I didn't know." He didn't pull away as she trailed her palms against his forearms.

He closed his eyes, settling into the warmth that flowed from her fingertips. His voice was soft and low when he spoke. "Things were hard for us after that. Our mother, Mary, never got over the loss. She did the best she could raising the four of us alone, but she couldn't get past our father being gone."

"Did they ever find his killer?" Stella asked.

Brennan hesitated before answering. "It took years

before they captured the man that murdered him," he said finally. "Everything about my father's case was why we all went into law enforcement. We wanted to uphold dad's memory through our work in the justice system and get as many criminals as we could off the streets. My father's killer was on death row when he got into a fight with a prison guard and was killed."

When he opened his eyes and lifted them to hers, Stella was staring at him intently. Compassion dampened her lashes, and her stare was like the sweetest balm.

"When you started calling me, I thought you were doing a story on my father's case. Over the years, we've had a lot of reporters wanting to interview us. It's not a story I was interested in sharing with the public. I didn't want to revisit the details of the case, and I didn't want my mother to have to relive dad's killing over again."

"No," she said. "I didn't know any of this. I called because I was hoping to get a lead on the Landmark Killer case. Something no one knew that could set my story apart from the other stories being written."

"A journalist through and through. I respect that." He trailed his hand down the side of her face, outlining her profile with his fingertips. He brushed a loose strand of hair away, tucking it gently behind her ear. The intimate gesture gave them both pause.

"Don't be facetious," Stella said, her voice a loud whisper.

Brennan's bright smile washed over her, lifting her spirit.

"I know you said your mom is in Florida now. Are you two close?" she asked, wanting to know as much about him as she could discover.

He nodded. "I adore my mother. We all visit her a few times during the year, and I speak with her weekly. When I'm going through something, I might call her every day just to hear her voice."

Stella smiled. "That's a blessing. I miss hearing my mother's voice."

He pulled her hand into his and kissed the back of her fingers. "I told my mom about you. When you were in the hospital, I kept her updated every day. I was afraid that I might lose you. I knew that she would pray for you when she went to Mass, and she did. She's still praying for you. And for us."

Stella lifted her brow, surprise painting her expression. "Brennan, I don't know what to say," she whispered.

He shrugged his shoulders. "You don't need to say anything, Stella. I just wanted you to know…" he started to say.

Before he could finish his comment, Stella lifted herself up and wrapped her arms around his neck. She pressed her mouth to his and captured his lips with her own. She kissed him hungrily, every ounce of feeling she had for the man exploding in a kiss that would forever leave them tied to each for an eternity.

It would be the first of many kisses. The connection so magnanimous that both could feel a cosmic shift of sorts, pulling air and space into a single thread that only they shared. Brennan knew he would never again be kissed by any woman with the level of desire he and Stella had for each other. He needed her. Badly. Like he needed oxygen and food. She became all his needs and his wants; the intensity of what was happening more than he could have ever imagined.

Stella tasted like a sweet syrup with a hint of banana from the pudding they had shared. Her mouth was sugar and heated, burning like a freshly lit torch. He wanted to hold her close and never let her go, and yet the intensity of them together was so exhilarating, he thought he might cry.

Time stood still. Sound was nonexistent, save their breath as both panted heavily. Her hands were hot, as were his, and they trailed paths across each other's body that burned every hope and dream each had into bare skin. Brennan pulled at her clothes, his own already lost to the floor. He pulled her against him, desperate to feel her bare flesh atop his own. He wrapped his arms tightly around her, his limbs like vices locked into play.

Stella moved with him in a seductive dance that left nothing to the imagination. She was dynamite exploding through nerve endings. She was snow melting on a mountain top. Stella was love in its purest form, and everything about her left Brennan whole and broken, confident and scared, forceful and timid. He was suddenly a contradiction of emotions, and he was famished for more.

Their kisses intensified, tongues easing past parted lips. Darting back and forth in a game of touch and treat. Kisses chased hands that led the way across skin damp from perspiration. Fingers pulled and pinched, and palms caressed and kneaded tissue that was soft and hard to the touch.

He kissed the curve of one breast and then the other, and suckled at nipples that had hardened like rock candy beneath his touch. Stella gasped. Or maybe he did. One echoed the other in a whispered mating cry. Every muscle in his body hardened, his blood vessels taut with anticipation. Stella sheathed him with a condom that seemed to appear out of thin air. Her touch, soft fingers wrapping around his hardened appendage moved him to quiver and shudder with anticipation, seconds from his entire body erupting like Hawaii's Mauna Loa volcano.

She eased above him and plunged her body down against his. Someone cried out in pure ecstasy, the sound like music wafting through the late-night air. Brennan bit down against his bottom lip to hold back the tears. They met each other stroke for stroke, a give and take so delicately balanced that no one and nothing could have torn them from each other.

Stella came first, murmuring his name over and over again as if in prayer. She pulled him with her as she plunged off the edge of ecstasy into a cavern of sheer bliss. Brennan screamed, his toes curling, his limbs cramping with pleasure. Everything between them exploded, firing fragments of sheer happiness through nerve endings. They were pure, unadulterated joy.

Their loving took them from room to room throughout the house. They made love in the kitchen, on the staircase, in the shower and on the guest room floor. It finally led them to Stella's bedroom and her king-sized bed.

Their sensual exploration lasted most of the night, occasional naps only coming as long as it took one or the other to catch their collective breath. When all was done, nothing else to learn and discover before the sun rose and reality swept in like a tidal wave, Stella lay her head against Brennan's chest. He wrapped himself tightly around her and held her close. Sleep tiptoed in, determined to reclaim its time as both drifted off into the sweetest dreams. Stella closed her eyes, her breathing and heart rate syncing in time with his. Brennan whispered her name, and then he said, I love you.

Stella had no idea the time. When she eased out of the bed to go to the bathroom, she only knew that it was still dark outside. Brennan was snoring softly beside her, and he rolled away, claiming the bed with the entirety of his body. She smiled at the sight of him, his wiry frame sprawled haphazardly against the pillow-topped mattress.

She like him there and that surprised her. She hated when a man thought he should spend the night in her bed after a sexual encounter. There had been shame when she had roused a lover and sent him on his way. Now, she hated the thought of Brennan leaving, and she realized that was a conversation to be had when all their bad business was behind them.

With an empty bladder, Stella eased back into the

room, settling down against the side of the bed. She had wrapped the length of her hair around her head and slipped on a silk bonnet to protect the strands. She was still thinking about what Brennan had said as they'd fallen off to sleep. Wondering if she had heard him correctly, or if her own wants and wishes had teased their way into her dreams. Because she wanted him to love her, and she wished things between them could always be what they were in that moment. When neither was crazed about their careers and no one was trying to kill her or cause him and his family harm.

Chapter 12

Brennan had broken every professional rule that had followed him since the day he'd gone into law enforcement. He'd been standing in the doorway for a while, watching as Stella slumbered. He still didn't know how he'd managed to get out of the bed without waking her, period. They had been entwined so tightly around each other that he could barely tell when her appendages ended and his began. But he had, rising from the mattress without disturbing her rest.

He closed his eyes and leaned against the door frame. He'd been there to protect her. Instead, he'd crossed the boundaries his job and her case had demanded of him. What he had done was cause for dismissal, and there wasn't anything he could do if the director called him on his behavior.

Brennan pounded his fist against his forehead. Crossing the line had been one thing. And then he'd added insult to injury by telling her that he loved her. He had known better, but the words had slipped off his tongue before he could catch them.

Despite all the things they had discussed over the past few weeks, the two had never talked about his aversion to a permanent relationship. He had no interest in marriage or anything that resembled it. Brennan had always been committed to his work, setting his personal life on a back burner to those cases that required his total focus. He had purposely dated women who were only looking for Mr. Right Now, no interest in a Mr. Right. It made things easier when he'd been ready to walk away. He had always kept his head in the game, successfully ensuring he kept his heart out of his encounters. Now, Stella Maxwell had a vicelike grip on his heart and his head, the woman stealing into every wakening thought he was having.

They had spent their time together, becoming fast friends and that friendship had him seriously considering what forever could possibly look like. Brennan didn't know how to handle all the emotions flooding his spirit. That damn text had thrown him completely offsides, leaving him angry and frustrated. Reflecting back on those memories of his father and that time in life when he and his family had been most broken, painful and sad. Sharing all of that with Stella had left him feeling vulnerable. Then a simple touch and a heated kiss had opened his heart to emotions he had never experienced before. He was feeling like an unholy mess, and redemption was nowhere to be found.

Taking a step back, Brennan closed the bedroom door. He stood for a moment to consider his options, and then he grabbed his bags and headed for the front door.

When Stella woke next, the sun was shining brightly through her bedroom windows. The temperature had risen, warning of a hot, blistering New York day. The bedroom door was closed, and Brennan was nowhere to be found. She wished he'd woken her, but she knew he still worried about her getting enough rest.

Rising, she headed toward the bathroom and the shower, anxious to be with Brennan after the incredible night they'd had shared. An hour later, she bounded eagerly down the steps, calling his name as she moved into the kitchen.

"Brennan! I was just thinking…" she started to say, expecting him to be standing as he did every morning—with a cup of coffee in his hands as breakfast awaited her. But there was no sign of him. No coffee brewed. No eggs or pancakes plated atop the stove.

She peered out to the rear patio first, then peeked through the front blinds. A patrol car remained parked in front, but Brennan's car was gone. Without giving it a second thought, Stella bounded back up the steps and into the guest bedroom. All things Brennan were gone, nothing belonging to the man to be found. Moving back into the hallway, she slid down the wall to the floor, pulling her knees to her chest.

Her stomach flipped, threatening to spew even though she hadn't yet eaten.

Brennan had left without even saying good-bye. There wasn't a note or a sign that what had happened had meant something to him. She'd been played, and she hadn't seen it coming.

Brennan had hidden in his office for most of the morning. He felt like a complete schmuck for leaving Stella the way he had. He kept looking at his cell phone, hoping she'd call to cuss him out, but she'd gone radio silent. He considered calling her but knew he couldn't begin to explain how he was feeling. He knew Stella would have had no interest in hearing how he was relationship shy. Instead, he called the patrol team staked out in front of her home. Once they confirmed she was still there, inside and safe, he was able to breathe easier.

A knock on the office door pulled at his attention. He looked up as his brother entered the room.

"What's going on?" Cash asked. He dropped into the empty seat in front of the large wooden desk. The two men exchanged a look.

"Nothing's going on. Why do you ask?" Brennan answered.

"Because you haven't been in your office since you took on that other case. Now you're here at the crack of dawn? Something's going on!"

"Why are you here so early?"

"Don't change the subject, big brother. What happened?"

Brennan shook his head. Contrition was like a heavy mask on his face. He didn't need to say it out loud. Twin intuition said it for him. The two men held a silent conversation, everything spilling over in their facial expressions.

Cash shook his head. "What the hell were you thinking?"

"I wasn't thinking. I was responding and it just happened." Brennan's voice was low as he spoke, concerned someone might overhear their conversation.

"How does Stella feel about it?" Cash asked.

Brennan shrugged. "I didn't talk to her before I left."

His brother's eyes widened. "Did you at least say good-bye?"

Brennan winced.

"Dude! Are you trying to purposely ruin things?"

"It's complicated."

"You ran. That's not hard to figure out. But I'm trying to figure out why? Clearly, you have feelings for Stella. We all saw that last night. You care about her. That's not complicated at all."

"Why are you really here? I know it's not to discuss my personal life."

Cash shook his head. "That text you received originated from a burner phone. The transmission signal was roaming from someplace on the West Coast. We can't track it. Whoever this is, he's good. His technical proficiency puts him a caliber above Ashlyn's, and that's saying something."

"Have you been here working on that all night?"

"Most of it. I didn't have anyone to canoodle with, so I worked."

Brennan gave his twin a look and chuckled softly as Cash shrugged his shoulders in jest.

"What do I do?" Brennan asked, looking completely befuddled.

Cash shook his head. "My only serious relationship crashed and burned big time," he said, reminded of the divorce that had broken up his family. "I'm not sure you should be asking me that question."

"Well, I am asking," Brennan replied.

"Talk to her. You will never get anywhere with her if the two of you stop communicating."

The stereo system was playing loudly through the home's speakers as Stella changed her clothes. She was singing along with the King George tune "Keep on Rollin'." She considered it her personal theme song, the lyrics saying one setback would not impede one's progress.

Her voice was crystal clear as she sang loudly.

She thought back to those days when her parents had danced to different songs, the two laughing as if neither had a care in the world. Those had been good days. After her mother died, her father would sometimes play a classic song as he stared out the window, the memories lifting his dark face into a slight smile.

She would never admit it out loud, but her heart hurt. Brennan had fractured it, leaving her feeling tattered. She'd fallen for the man. She had allowed him in, and he had left her devastated. Stella also knew the best way to come back from that kind of hurt was to throw herself into her work. So, unless the *New York Wire* was prepared to officially fire her, Stella was done and finished with her leave of absence. She was going back to work.

She continued to sing.

Brennan and Cash were still talking. His cousin Sinead had joined them. Reviewing all the details of the case for the umpteenth time, they were plotting their next steps. His phone ringing interrupted the conversation.

"Agent Colton."

The speaker's response was muffled, but Sinead and Cash shot each other a look, Brennan's expression cause for concern.

"Yes… When? Did she say where she was going? Thank you," he said, disconnecting the call. Frustration looked like bad makeup across his face.

"Stella left the house and blew off the security team," he said.

"Why would she do that?" Sinead questioned.

"Yes, Brennan," Cash said facetiously, "why would Stella do that?"

Brennan glared at his twin. Sinead looked from one to the other and back.

"What did you do?" she suddenly asked, resting her stare on Brennan.

"Let it go," her cousin answered, rising from his seat.

Sinead looked at Cash, who eagerly answered her question.

"He slept with her. Then he snuck out of the house

like a thief. He didn't even say good-bye to her. Just packed his bags and left. He hit it and quit it!"

Sinead glared at Brennan. "Please tell me you did not to that to that woman! How can you be such an ass?"

Brennan stood up. "I really don't need this from you two. I need to go and find Stella."

"Did they know where she was going?" Cash asked.

"No, but I think I do," Brennan answered. He fell into thought. He knew Stella well and would have bet his last dollar that she was headed to her job. He needed to meet her there to apologize and to convince her to go back home, where she was safe.

A knock on the door stalled his thoughts. Xander opened the door and peered inside. He was breathing heavy, as if he'd been running.

"You okay, dude?" Brennan questioned.

"I took the stairs," Xander said with a nod. "Sorry to interrupt, but a call just came in. There has been another shooting. You all are up."

"Where?" Cash queried.

"The Capstone Theater. The victim is a man named Landon Stone. NYPD will meet you there. They've sent you the location."

"Thank you," Brennan said, scrolling through the messages on his phone. "The victim is still alive," he said as he grabbed his suit jacket. "I'm going to meet Rory at the hospital."

"I'll run point here," Sinead said. "Just keep me in the loop."

Cash nodded. "I'll head over to Broadway to check out the crime scene."

"Damn!" Brennan muttered as they all rushed from the room. "The Landmark Killer has dropped another body in our laps. He's gotten his L for Maeve O'Leary."

"I'll update Director Chang," Xander said, calling after them. Then he closed the office door as he watched them disappear into the field.

"Ms. Maxwell! It's good to see you!" The senior editor for the *Wire* was a man named Brian Price. He was lean and lanky, like he'd played basketball his whole life. To hear him tell it, though, he had no aptitude at all for sports or anything athletic. His youthful appearance, sun-kissed complexion, blue-tipped hair and playful exuberance belied his sixty-plus years.

He jumped from his seat to shake Stella's hand. "We've missed you around here!"

Stella gave him a wry smile. Brian was notorious for blowing smoke at his employees. "And that's why I wanted to see you," she said. "I'm ready to return to work."

"You've been through a lot, Stella. Are you sure it's not too soon?"

"I'm certain. I need to get back to my desk. I need to be writing."

"It's my understanding that you are still under police protection. Is that true?" He leaned forward in his seat, meeting her stare with a narrowed gaze.

"Where did you hear that?"

"An Agent Brennan Colton called about you a short while ago. He was quite concerned about your safety. It almost sounded personal," Brian said, the comment edged in curiosity.

Stella bristled. The nerve of him, she thought. Was Brennan trying to totally ruin her life? She took a deep breath. "I assure you, Brian, I'll be fine."

"But what about the other employees? There's already been one tragedy surrounding you. Can you assure me the rest of us are safe?"

Stella took another deep breath, blowing it out slowly. Unfortunately, she couldn't give him that assurance since they still had no clue who had targeted her. She'd been so focused on her own hurt that she hadn't stopped to consider that her being out and about could potentially put others in danger. She said, "I can easily work from home until there are no concerns. You can key me into meetings electronically, and I can still give you the stories I know you're looking for."

"Even the Colton story?"

"Excuse me?" Stella's brow lifted, his question throwing her off-kilter. "What Colton story?"

"I recognized Brennan Colton's name. He's one of the FBI agents working the Landmark Killer case. I also did a little research myself, and his father was murdered by a serial killer years ago. You can't tell me there's no story there. It could be an amazing human interest piece. And from the way he spoke, something tells me that you might have inside access. Imagine that story being scooped!"

"I'm not sure…" Stella started. Her eyes darted back and forth as she considered what he was asking of her. She might be mad at Brennan, but she would never consider betraying him or his family that way. Sure, there was a potential headline with the Colton family history, the details surrounding the patriarch's murder that led them all into law enforcement, specifically tracking down serial killers and the current murders being investigated. It could potentially be a huge headline for the right reporter. She would have gladly written that story weeks earlier. But now… now she had to consider the consequences of doing such a thing. Bottom line, even if Brennan Colton was a complete and total jerk, she loved him and would never consider doing anything to cause him harm.

"Let me help you make a decision," Brian said, grinning at her sheepishly. "We got a tip in that the Landmark Killer is sending anonymous text messages to the FBI team. The Coltons specifically."

"When did you hear this?" Stella asked. A deep frown pulled across her face.

"Someone sent that message to your inbox earlier today. Obviously, you not being here, I intercepted it. But I'm willing to give it back to you to chase down. Find out if it's true, connect it to the Coltons chasing down a killer and spill the tea on their personal connection. It's a hell of a story, Stella, and if you want to come back to work, it's all yours."

"And if I don't want that story?"

"Then you don't want this job," Brian said matter-of-factly. "But I'm willing to give you some time to think about it. Not too much though. Let's just say I'll need an answer in twenty-four hours."

With a quick nod, Stella exited the office, feeling out of sorts by the conversation. She suddenly wanted to be home, where she could shut herself off from the world. Her friend Garrett was standing outside her former cubicle waving at her excitedly.

"Stella!"

The two friends hugged, jumping up and down in each other's arms.

"It's so good to see you, Garrett!"

"Honey, I have been worried to death about you."

"I've been good actually."

"How did it go with Price?"

Stella rolled her eyes skyward. "Some things don't ever change. That son of a bitch is blackmailing me for my job."

"Price would auction off his firstborn for a story!" He leaned in, taking a quick glance to see who might be eavesdropping on their conversation. His voice dropped to a loud whisper.

"Word around the office is the new kid is gunning for your cubicle. He's been chasing down those stories you would normally do. If there's a story Price wants, you can bet he's already promised it to Junior Mafia thinking you wouldn't be around to take it."

She giggled. "Is that what you're calling him, Junior Mafia?"

"His name's Carmine Something or Other. He's a nice Italian boy whose grandfather supposedly worked for the Gambino crime family. Price hired him because he claimed he could dish about the mafia family's current enterprises."

"Has he?"

"He's chasing your stories, Stella. He has nothing of his own to share!"

"Well, I'm trying to come back to write my own stories, but Price is being a real butthole."

"How can I help?"

Stella sighed. "Not sure anyone can help me with this one," she said.

Stella appreciated Garrett taking time from his own schedule to sit and have lunch with her. She'd missed his crude jokes and laughter as they gossiped about others in the office. Although both kept looking over their shoulders for unaccompanied packages or ninjas driving paneled vans, it was a good time. The break from her usual routine also allowed her to clear her head and figure out what she wanted to do.

She dialed Brennan's number and waited for him to answer his cell phone. He picked up on the second ring.

"Stella, are you okay?"

"Please don't act like you really care."

"Stella, I'm sorry and I do care."

"I just thought you should know that someone emailed me at the *Wire* about the anonymous text messages from the Landmark Killer that you and your cousin received. My boss intercepted the message."

"How in the hell…?" Brennan stammered.

"My guess is whoever sent the messages is tipping off the media. My editor knows there's a story there, and he is sniffing hard to find it. Apparently, after you called to discuss me and my current situation with him, he did some digging into your past and found out about your father."

"You and I need to talk," Brennan said.

"No, we don't. You said everything you needed to say when you left this morning. It's no big deal."

"It is a big deal, but now's not a good time to have this conversation. And definitely not over the phone. There's been another shooting. The victim is still alive. I'm headed to the hospital now."

"Well, good luck with that," Stella said.

"Stella, please! I can meet you home as soon as I'm done here."

"You may be there most of the night. And I have things to do."

"I need to explain."

"Not necessary. We just had sex and then you booked it. You didn't even bother to thank me for the good time or say good-bye. There is nothing that you need to say to me now that I'm interested in hearing."

Brennan's voice dropped an octave. "First of all, we did not just have sex. I made love to you. It was so much more than some casual fling through your sheets."

"I wouldn't know. The way you packed up and took off didn't feel very loving."

"Dammit, Stella! I don't need this right now."

Slamming the phone down in Brennan's ear gave Stella much satisfaction. She refused to be moved, and she didn't care what he was in the middle of trying to resolve. They were done. She'd been nice enough to give him a heads-up about the information that was leaked. As far as she was concerned, she didn't owe Brennan Colton another minute of her time.

Brennan was pulling into the hospital parking lot when Stella disconnected the call. His frustration was palpable and he considered calling her back. Instead, he found a parking space and headed for the emergency room entrance. The New York Police Department had cordoned off the area, and as he approached the door, he flashed his badge. The rookie officer looked him up and down before allowing him to pass.

"Where can I find Detective Colton?" he asked another uniformed officer who was standing at the reception desk.

They pointed him toward the waiting room, the space bustling with activity. Rory stood off in a corner, texting messages to her team, who were still on sight.

"Hey," Brennan said as he moved to her side. "What do we have?"

"White male, midthirties, took a bullet to his left side, currently in critical condition. They just took him up to surgery."

"Are we sure it's our guy? Was there a note?"

"No note. He got spooked. Another employee heard the shot and interrupted him. The perp was standing over the body and took off running when she cried out for help. One guy gave chase but lost him in the crowd."

Rory paused, texting on her phone before she refocused and continued, "As soon as the doctors bring us that bullet, we'll run the ballistics for confirmation. Right now, though, everything is pointing toward our killer."

"If he's the L. And why is this guy going out of order if he's spelling Maeve O'Leary's name? Unless it's just to fool with us?"

Rory nodded. "Unfortunately, whatever's going on, Landon Stone's name didn't do him any favors. So now we have to wait and pray he pulls through."

"What about the woman who walked in on them?"

Rory looked down at her phone. "Cash is there interviewing her now. Her name is Gail Cooper. She told my guys that the killer wore a mask and had on a hoodie and baggy clothes. She didn't notice anything else. She said it was dark. Someone had shut down the stage lights, and Landon had gone to check the fuse box. That's why he was back there alone."

"If there's something more, Cash will get it from her."

"That's what I was thinking."

Brennan stole a glance toward his watch. Rory turned to take a seat and he followed. "We have another problem," he said as he made himself comfortable.

Rory's eyes lifted questioningly. "What now?"

"I just spoke to Stella. She said someone's tipped the *New York Wire* off about the anonymous messages Sinead and I received."

"Are they going to run it?"

"I don't know. I'm not sure if Stella knew anything either."

"She's a journalist. You don't think she wouldn't run the story?"

The question gave Brennan pause. He wouldn't think Stella would do something like that, but their circumstances had changed. And she was angry.

"I don't think so," he said finally.

"You do know you might not be able to trust a woman who you've royally pissed off, right?"

Brennan's head snapped in his cousin's direction.

Rory chuckled. "Don't look surprised. You know it's hard to keep secrets in this family."

He shook his head. "I don't know what to do. She won't talk to me."

"I wouldn't talk to you either. When did you become such a big jerk?"

He tossed up his hands in frustration. "I screwed up! I just want to make amends."

"What happens if she's not interested? Are you prepared to let her go?"

Shifting forward in his seat, Brennan dropped his head into his hands. With every question Rory asked, things were beginning to look bleaker and bleaker. He hadn't wanted to consider that things with him and Stella were over. He clearly hadn't been thinking at all.

Chapter 13

"Stella? Stella Maxwell? I thought that was you!"

Tensing, Stella looked up anxiously, surprised to hear her name being called. She hadn't expected to run into anyone in the Duane Reade Pharmacy. As Pamela Littlefield sauntered in her direction, she felt her entire body relax, realizing just how tense she had been.

"Pamela, hello!"

"How are you?"

"I'm doing well, thank you. How about yourself?"

"Busy as always. I'm so glad we ran into each other. I'd been planning to call you after that horrible incident at Rockwell's vigil. I hated that that happened to you." Pamela's smile was wide.

"I appreciate that. Things happen, though, when emotions are running high."

"Don't I know it!" Pamela said, waving a dismissive hand. "Things were crazy there for a while. I hear you had it rough too. That someone tried to blow you up? It was all in the news."

Stella shrugged. "Yes, it was."

"You'd think you being a reporter and all that you could do something about the stuff they write about you." Pamela's head was waving anxiously from side to side.

"You'd think," Stella responded. "Well, I need to finish my shopping and get going. It was nice to see you again."

"You didn't ask me what I've been doing," Pamela said, a hint of attitude in her tone.

Stella blinked, her lashes batting up and down rapidly. She took an inhale of air before she spoke. "Didn't I? I'm sorry about that. So, what's new with you?"

"The campaign keeps me busy, and you know what a tyrant Tobias can be. It's exhausting!" Pamela paused to take a breath. "Here," she said, reaching into her purse. "Have a campaign button!"

Stella held out her hand as Pamela dropped the button into her palm. "Marshall Tucker? That was quick."

"That's politics!" Pamela chirped. "But what I wanted to tell you is that I got engaged!" She held out her hand for Stella to see the engagement ring on her finger. It was a thin band with a petite stone, and it flattered her small hands.

"Congratulations! How exciting!"

Exuberance wrapped itself around Pamela like a wool blanket. "We haven't set a date yet for the wedding. I think we should wait until after the election, but my fiancée doesn't want to wait."

"I'm sure you'll both figure out the perfect time."

"It's so sad that you and Rockwell never got engaged. But things happen for a reason. Right?"

Stella gave her a polite nod, wanting to cut the conversation short. "Well, I'm glad we could catch up. But I really do have to run. It was good to see you and hear your good news."

Pamela smiled widely a second time. "It was. You take care, and I look forward to our seeing each other again soon. Maybe we can do lunch?"

"I'll keep that in mind," Stella said. "Maybe when our schedules aren't so busy, especially with the election and all."

"You're right. But soon, okay?"

"Okay! Bye now!" Stella grabbed her basket and headed toward the register. She could feel Pamela's stare still locked on her. She was curious to know what the woman was doing in that neighborhood but decided that to ask would take more time than she had to spare.

For a brief moment, she considered calling Brennan to tell him about the encounter but remembered their relationship wasn't like that anymore. By the time she'd finished purchasing the tampons, clear nail polish, deodorant and face cream she'd selected, she'd decided there really wasn't anything for her to be concerned about. She and Pamela had never had a problem with each other before. She couldn't imagine that anything had changed.

Minutes later, she made her exit, heading toward the subway station. Pamela stood on the corner, hailing a yellow cab. She waved and called out good-bye one last time. Stella waved back and hurried in the opposite direction. She couldn't get home fast enough.

Hours later, Stella was pacing from room to room. She'd been there long enough to check the locks at least a half dozen times and had actually checked them a dozen times more. It surprised her that she was as anxious as she was. Going out had seemed like a good idea that morning, but as she had come to realize how exposed she was, that good idea had felt wholeheartedly foolish. She was kicking herself for acting so irrationally simply because her feelings had been hurt.

She moved into the kitchen, trying to decide what to make herself for dinner. Suddenly, the prospect of eating alone felt like a challenge. She moved to the wine chiller, grabbed the first bottle she touched, popped the cork and took a swig. Leaning back against the refrigerator, warm tears suddenly misted her eyes.

She hated that she had grown comfortable with Brennan. Hated that he had made her feel safe. She found it galling that she had actually thought there was something special between them, and it infuriated her that she'd given herself to him and that she hadn't protected her heart.

Now her own shadow was scaring her. Bumping into old acquaintances felt sketchy, and she no longer trusted her own judgment. In the blink of an eye, she felt as if she'd been taken advantage of. Brennan had used her, and she had let him.

Stella had started her day happy and hopeful. Minutes later, it had gone straight to hell. Now she hurt, someone still wanted to cause her harm and everything she'd believed in felt lost to her. Taking another swallow of wine, Stella leaned across the counter and cried.

Brennan was certain he'd worn through the soles off his leather shoes with all the pacing he had done. It had been a long afternoon waiting for news on the latest victim. Waiting to see if the man would survive was physically draining. It had left him with nothing else to do but think. And with no new leads to follow, all that was on his mind was Stella.

He still couldn't believe he'd walked out on her the way he had. She had trusted him, and he had failed her. He couldn't blame her if she never wanted to have anything else to do with him. If she refused to give him a second chance, he wasn't certain he even deserved one.

Brennan would never be able to explain how he was feeling because even he didn't understand the wealth of emotion that was suddenly so consuming. All he knew was that he wanted to go home. Home was wherever Stella was, and he'd managed to burn down the walls the two had built together.

He loved Stella and he had told her so. If he could tell her again, he would. But Stella wasn't having any of it, and now he worried for her safety. Worried about her being well, and he was petrified things between them had ended before they'd had a chance to let the relationship bloom.

Rory suddenly called his name, interrupting those thoughts. She gestured toward the doctor who was headed in their direction. Both shifted their focus, giving the physician their undivided attention. Rory flashed her badge and introduced them.

"How's Mr. Stone doing?" Brennan questioned.

Dr. Ralph Brett nodded. "Under the circumstances, he's doing amazingly well. He's a very lucky man. The bullet just missed his lungs. An eighth of an inch in either direction, and things would be very different for him."

"We're going to need that bullet," Rory said.

The doctor nodded. "I bagged it. We just need your signature on the paperwork for the chain of custody."

"Not a problem," Rory replied.

"When can we speak with Mr. Stone?" Brennan asked.

"Not before tomorrow. He's just gone down to recovery and will probably spend the night in the ICU so we can keep our eye on him. If things go well, you should be able to talk to him in the morning."

"Thank you, Doctor," Rory said.

The two stood and watched as the man walked away.

"I swear," Brennan said. "We can't catch a damn break!"

Rory shrugged. "I'm going back to the crime scene. Let's regroup here in the morning."

Brennan said, "Sounds like a plan. Let me know if anything else comes up. I'll also give Cash a call to see if he got anywhere."

"Will do," Rory replied. "And Brennan...?"

"Yes?"

"Go make things right with Stella!"

Brennan had been standing on her porch for at least ten minutes knocking at the door. Stella was conflicted as she peered at him through the front window. She wanted to let him in. And she wanted to tell him to go to hell. She watched as he moved down the steps to have a conversation with a uniformed officer standing on the sidewalk. Their exchange was brief before Brennan came back to the door and rang the bell again.

Stella took a deep breath and moved to the entrance. She opened the door slightly and looked out. "What do you want, Brennan?" she asked, attitude wrapped around every word.

"I wanted to make sure you were okay."

"I'm fine."

"We need to talk."

"Say what you have to say."

"Can I come in, Stella?"

"No."

"We need to have a conversation about your case. You're going to lose the security team after tomorrow. We've finally hit that shortfall in the NYPD budget.

We should talk about other options, maybe consider private security for the time being. At least until we can be certain you are safe."

Stella winced. After the day she'd had, that was the last thing she wanted to hear. Her anxiety rose a level.

Brennan persisted. "Stella, please, let me come inside!"

"I don't want you in my house. I can't trust you," she said.

Brennan blew a soft sigh. "That's fair and I understand, but we can't fix this if you don't give us a chance."

"We? Us? I'm sorry, I didn't walk out on you. I was here for a conversation this morning. You weren't. I don't need to fix anything, and clearly, *we* never existed."

"I was scared, Stella. And I made a mistake."

There was a moment of pause, and then Stella said, "That's not my problem."

A heavy gust of warm breath blew past Brennan's thin lips. He took another breath and held it deep in his lungs before exhaling again. "What do you want from me, Stella?" he asked.

"Not a damn thing!" Stella answered. "I don't want one damn thing from you, Brennan Colton!"

"Please, Stella…" Brennan started to say.

Eyeing him one last time, Stella shook her head, then closed and locked her door.

Brennan returned to the office to clean up some paperwork. He had hoped to be spending time with

Stella, making up for his transgression. He would have cooked a special dinner, let her pick a movie for them to watch and massaged her feet as they lay on the sofa together. It would have been relaxing and joyful, the two continuing to discover each other's eccentricities. He had really wanted things to be well between them. He'd practically been desperate for it.

Stella however had no intentions of making it easy for him. And that was okay, he thought. He was willing to work as hard as he needed to if it meant things between them could be well again. There was just something about her that made him happy. Even in the midst of so much sorrow and frustration, Stella Maxwell was the sweetest ray of sunshine. Even when she was being surly and giving him a hard time.

He packed away the folders on top of the desk, and when it was clear, he made his exit, turning the lights off behind him. The office was quiet at that hour, only a few agents still working out problems or finishing up paperwork. As he headed toward the exit, Xander waved him down, hurrying out of the director's office.

"Brennan, I'm glad I caught you! For some reason I thought you'd already left."

"I did. I went and grabbed a slice of pizza for dinner and came back. What's up?"

"I received a call this afternoon from a reporter at the *New York Wire*. They wanted a statement about you and your work. They asked questions about your past, as well as your record here with the bureau. I told them no comment and then referred them to the bureau's public communications department. They handle all that. I just thought you should know."

Brennan hesitated as he considered the consequences of the media digging into his life. When his father had been killed, they'd been relentless, harassing his mother and them like blood hounds running after a catch. Then there had been the daily headlines and strangers staring at them like they were exhibits at the zoo. School had been the worst, other kids relentless with the questions and bullying. What had happened to his family had been emotionally debilitating, and he'd be damned if he allowed it to happen to them again.

"Thank you," Brennan said. "I appreciate you looking out."

"Just doing my job. You have a good night!"

"You too, Xander. You too!"

Brennan needed to clear his head, so he walked. Why he'd chosen to walk Broadway remained to be answered. But he loved the city at night. It grounded him, and there was actually something magical about the late-night atmosphere. The lights were abundant, casting shadows across the streets and buildings, and most people out that time of night had either left a good time or were heading to one. Rarely did he ever run into anyone who wasn't simply minding their own business, not bothering him as long as he didn't bother them.

The consequences of what he'd done had slapped him broadside. It had been in the look Stella had given him, the harshness of her tone, punctuated by that door closing in his face. He'd been taken aback, believing that an apology would have been enough to make amends for any of his actions. But he now realized that his actions had cut deep, and there was still an open wound that hadn't even begun to heal. He'd messed up, and Stella didn't mind making sure he knew it.

Brennan crossed the street to walk the other sidewalk. His mind wouldn't rest. Two killers were out here still able to wreak havoc when they least expected. If there was nothing else he was certain of, he was certain that they would strike again. He hated feeling like he was being toyed with; a puppet of sorts who could only react when something happened.

With each step, he revisited one case and then the other, going over what they knew again and again. The Landmark Killer's last victim had survived. That added a new dimension to the case. They had to consider how he'd respond. Would he go after Landon Stone a second time? Would he pick another victim to kill, determined that he stay on task with his body count? What would he do? And when?

Rockwell Henley's killer hadn't surfaced since the bombing. Had their obsession with Stella changed, or were they waiting? Sitting back knowing that time would be their friend and she would become comfortable again, no longer wary of people. Did the unintended deaths of the postal worker and the patrol officer strike a chord, playing on their sensibility?

Did they have regrets that pushed them to let their obsession go?

The thoughts in his head were circling much like he was walking from New York block to New York block. His late-night stroll would inevitably come to an end as he made his way home or back to the office, depending on his mood. But the noise in his head had taken up permanent residency, and there was nothing that would change that except solving both cases efficiently and effectively so that convictions were guaranteed.

Stella bolted upright in her bed. A loud bang had sounded through the room, pulling her from a light sleep. She sat for a moment and listened for any other strange noises before throwing her legs off the side of the bed. When her feet hit the floor, her toe slammed into her iPad, and she realized she had knocked it off the bed and onto the floor as she'd slept. A wave of relief flooded through her.

Rising, she eased down the steps to peer outside. The patrol car was still parked out front. Learning that would soon end had left her jumpy. She wasn't ready to admit that she was outright scared. She tried hard to pretend that she was okay after watching two men be blown up in front of her. She'd successfully convinced herself that a masked gang trying to drag her off to no-man's-land was no big deal. Just a single bad day in a line of ordinary days. She knew she wasn't fooling anyone, but it helped to pretend like she was.

After grabbing a glass of water, she eased back

up the stairs and settled down in her bed. Pretending she didn't miss Brennan felt harder to pull off, because she would have given anything to have him there with her. Curling up against him to fall asleep would have been a dream come true, and she no longer believed in happily ever after.

The *New York Wire* wanted a story about him and his family and their connection to so much bad business. They wanted her to write it, and Stella would if it was anyone but Brennan. Or could she? Would it be better coming from her, a woman who knew him intimately or some random stranger who didn't care about him? And what if she refused? Where would that leave her career?

Being angry with him was proving to be harder than she'd imagined, and she had never before had a problem walking away from relationship that wasn't working for her. But she didn't want to walk away. She wanted to give him a hard shake and then make love to him like that first time.

Everything was complicated in a way that Stella didn't know how to resolve. Who hated her so much that they would go to such lengths to harm her? Why wasn't the puzzle falling into place, the whodunit ending on a high note, like in the movies? How much longer could she pretend not to be concerned? And why wasn't she certain about how things with Brennan would play out? Could they continue to be friends? Friends with benefits? Or was it possible that love would be everything the two desired? Or even more disturbing, what if she couldn't get past the hurt for things to be well with them again? What if she wrote that story and he hated her for doing so? What if this stall was just the beginning of one serious crash and burn?

Chapter 14

When Stella stepped out of the elevators in the *New York Wire* building, Garrett was there to greet her. Her friend grabbed her arm and pulled her down the hall toward the administrative offices.

"What's going on?" Stella asked, her eyes wide.

"I just want to wish you luck and prepare you. They plan to dangle a promotion in front of you for the inside scoop on that Colton family. And one of those fools down in marketing started a pool for everyone to bet on whether or not you'd do it."

Stella rolled her eyes skyward. "These people make me sick!"

Garrett smirked. "Full disclosure… I did put in my twenty dollars. The pot's almost a thousand bucks right now!"

"What did you bet?"

"I'm not going to tell you. I don't want to influence your decision. Just don't disappoint a friend!"

Stella laughed. "You make me sick!"

"Hey, I like to think that if anyone around here knows you, I know you best."

"You're lucky I love you, Garrett, because I'm not in a good mood this morning. I really don't want to have this conversation. I just want to come back to work."

"It'll be okay. You've got this," Garrett said. He leaned to give her a hug. "I've got an interview, so I need to run. I'll keep my fingers crossed that it all works out in your favor. I miss having you around."

Garrett gave her a wink and headed in the opposite direction. Taking a deep breath, Stella headed toward the senior editor's office.

"Stella Maxwell!" Brian's grin was Cheshire-cat wide as he popped up out of his chair to greet her. He pumped her arm up and down excitedly, then pointed her to a seat. Returning to his own, he leaned across the desk, his hands folded together in front of him.

"I knew you wouldn't disappoint me! So, what's you're angle on the story?"

"I have no angle," Stella said. "In fact, I'm only here to tell you that it's not a story I'm interested in writing."

Brian looked surprised, his wide smile falling into a deep frown. "How can you not be interested? This could be an award-winning piece, and with your personal connection to Brennan Colton…"

Stella bristled, a wave of surprise washing over her complexion. "What do you mean, 'personal connection'?"

"I mean, he's practically living with you, right?" Brian smiled again. "We've been getting some interesting information. I'm sure with everything you know and my tips, it'll fill in a lot of blanks and connect the dots."

"Who's giving you these tips, Brian?" Stella questioned.

"That's on a need-to-know basis, and you don't need to know if you don't plan to work here."

"Brian, I can only reiterate how much I love my job. And I'm good at it. In fact, I'm one of the best journalists to work at this rag. I'm ready to come back. But I will not write the article you want. I don't think there's a story there. At least not one that our readership will be interested in. I think there are other stories and angles I can get behind that will be far more lucrative for the paper."

"But that's the only headline I want," Brian said snidely, "whether you write it or not. We're here to get the news out, Stella, not protect your boyfriend. You need to decide what's more important to you—this job or that man."

The silence that suddenly descended over the room was thundering. When Stella finally spoke, her voice was low and even, just the faintest hint of hostility in her tone.

"Brian, I'm a journalist. I report news, not gossip. That *man* and I have no personal connection. He is *not* my boyfriend. But what's most important to me is maintaining my journalistic integrity. Because whether I work here or somewhere else, my integrity will follow wherever I go. Clearly, you should want to do the same. So my answer is still no."

"Then why are you here?" Brian snapped. He leaned back in his seat and crossed his arms over his torso. His jaw had tightened, and a blood vessel in his neck was pulsating as if it were preparing to burst.

Stella hesitated, seeming to drift off into thought as she considered his question. Finally, she lifted her eyes to meet his stare. "I'm just here to pack up my desk and say good-bye," she said, rising from the chair she'd taken a seat in.

"You'll regret this, Stella!" Brian yelled as she moved to the door and made her exit. "Trust me when I tell you, you will regret this."

"Not nearly as much as you will, Brian" Stella replied.

Stella had quit her job. She was still stunned that things went as far left as quickly as they had. Clearly, Brian hadn't been interested in her ever returning to her job, and that told her everything she needed to know about working for the *New York Wire*.

She blew out a soft sigh. Garrett helped her pack her few belongings as a security guard stood watch over the computer. He'd been giddy about her turning the assignment down, having wanted the office pool to fall in his favor. But he brought her to tears with his good-bye, reminding her why she loved her job and would miss seeing him on a daily basis.

"You're not getting rid of me that easy," Garrett said.

"We have a standing lunch date every Thursday at one o'clock. Thai…until I get tired of it, and then we'll pick a new spot. So don't be late."

"What if I get tired of Thai food first?"

"We'll talk about it. But I'll still have a job to go back to. Things will need to be convenient for me."

Stella laughed. "That was low! Even for you, Garrett."

"But it made you laugh!"

She slid the photograph of her parents into the container and slid on the lid. She took one last glance around the space and nodded. "I won't be bullied or blackmailed," she said, the comment not directed at anyone in particular.

Garrett nodded. His voice dropped an octave, and his tone changed, the joviality waning ever so slightly. "I'm proud of you. They don't deserve you, Stella! So, when you get that job working for the *New York Times*, remember who your friends were. I might need you to put in a good word for me."

She smiled. "What if I go to the *Washington Post*?"

He chuckled heartily. "Forget you know me. I have no plans to ever leave New York City!"

Stella winked her eye at her friend. "Neither do I!"

Brennan and Rory stood outside of hospital room 413 waiting to speak with Landon Stone. Their entry had been barred by a nurse, whose petite frame made her look like Tinker Bell, but with her attitude, she came across like a sumo wrestler, larger than life and potentially deadly. Brennan had learned early in life not to mess with women like that, and even Rory admitted to being slightly intimidated.

"Did she snap her finger at us?" Rory asked as the door closed in their faces.

Brennan nodded his head. Not only had she snapped her finger, but she'd also given them a look that could have melted ice.

"Should I knock?"

"I don't think so," Brennan said. "Do you have the doctor's direct number in your phone?"

"That won't be necessary," a stern voice said, interrupting their conversation. "Mr. Stone is ready to speak with you. But don't take too long. He needs his rest," the nurse said, peeking out the door at the two of them.

Brennan smiled. "Thank you."

The nurse opened the door to let them enter, and then she exited the space, closing the door behind her.

Landon Stone looked like a man who'd just been shot and undergone emergency surgery. He was hooked to multiple monitors and lay back in the bed with his eyes closed. His complexion was ashen, not an ounce of color in his cheeks. But his blond hair had been brushed neatly into place, and when he did open his eyes to look at them, they were a brilliant shade of radiant blue.

Rory took the lead. "Mr. Stone, my name is Detective Rory Colton. I'm with the NYPD, investigating your attempted murder. This is FBI Special Agent Brennan Colton, and we're both with the team investigating your assault. We apologize for disturbing your rest, but it's important that we ask you some questions."

Landon Stone nodded, looking from one to the other. He cleared his voice before he spoke. "I don't know what I can tell you," he said softly, his voice a loud whisper.

"Can you tell us what was going on before you were shot?" Brennan asked.

Landon closed his eyes again, his breathing slightly labored. They waited until he was ready to speak. It was only a few seconds, but it felt like forever. Brennan took a deep breath when he finally opened his eyes.

"We were…finishing up…rehearsal," he said, "when the lights…went out."

He took a deep breath and then continued, "I knew…where the…the…fuse box was. So I volunteered…to go check."

"Was it dark back there also?" Rory asked.

He nodded ever so slightly. "The back door…was open, and there was light…coming through."

"Is that door always left open?" Brennan questioned.

"No."

"What happened next?" Brennan said.

"I saw…something move. And…when I looked… there was a man."

Rory shot Brennan a look. "You're certain it was a man?"

Landon nodded his head, his blue eyes closing and

then opening again. "Yes. But he had on a mask. And dark clothes."

"Was he large? Small?"

"He had on a…a mask. A carnival mask…like for Mardi…Mardi Gras."

"Did he say anything? Or speak to you?"

"He said a name… May…or Mary…"

"Could it have been Maeve?" Rory asked.

"That's it…and the last…last name was Irish. O something…like…like O'Malley."

"Then what happened?" Brennan said.

"He shot me!" Landon gasped, and when he did, one of his monitors beeped loudly. At the same time, the blood pressure cuff around his arm activated.

"Do you remember anything after that?" Brennan said, persisting.

Landon paused. "He had…nice…nice shoes."

The room door swung open, and Landon's nurse stormed inside. "Time's up. Mr. Stone needs to get his rest."

"Why did you notice his shoes?" Brennan asked, ignoring her.

Landon waved a weak hand. "I was…I was… lying on the floor…and he…was standing…next to me. They were leather…and expensive…"

"I said—" the nurse started to say.

Rory rolled her eyes at the woman. "Thank you for your time, Mr. Stone."

Seconds later, the two had been shuffled back into the hallway. Nurse Pain in the Ass was standing at the nurse's station eyeing the two of them, venom shooting from her stare.

"I need a distraction," Brennan said.

"What are you…?" Rory started to say, the words catching in her chest as he glared at her with a narrowed gaze.

With a shake of her head, Rory moved to the nurse's station, asking questions that pulled the woman's attention from him. When the two were focused elsewhere, he moved back into the room to Landon Stone's bedside.

"Landon, I have one more question," he said, rousing the man from the lull of sleep.

Landon opened his eyes, a hint of curiosity peering up at Brennan.

"I need to show you some images. Would you let me know if you recognize any of them?"

Landon nodded his head slowly.

Brennan pulled seven photographs from the inner pocket of his suit jacket. One by one he showed them to Landon. One by one Landon shook his head no.

"Thank you," Brennan said. "I'll get out of your way this time. I promise"

"Just catch him," Landon said, his voice slightly stronger.

Brennan nodded. "Yes, sir. That's my goal."

Stepping back into the hallway, Brennan appreciated that Rory was still chattering away. The nurse was clearly beginning to lose her patience. He gestured for Rory's attention and turned, heading toward the bank of elevators at the end of the hallway.

"What was that about?" she asked when they were inside the elevator.

Brennan passed her the stack of photographs. "I was hoping he might have recognized someone."

The images were staff members from the 130th precinct and the FBI office. They were persons the team had named when they were last together at Stella's house. Potential suspects who might be killing to honor Maeve O'Leary and taunting the Colton family for the hell of it. Landon not recognizing any of them was disheartening.

Rory flipped through the lot of them, and then she burst out laughing, pulling one in particular from the pile. "Did you really include a picture of Cash?"

"Why not?"

"What if he had picked your twin brother out of the stack?" Rory said, still giggling.

Brennan laughed. "Then we'd really have a problem!"

"Where now?" his cousin asked. They had exited the building, heading to the parking area.

Brennan paused, considering their options. The conversation with Landon hadn't given them anything new to work with. They were still at a complete loss. He turned to give Rory a look.

"Let's go to Rikers. I want to talk to Maeve."

Stella had a lengthy list of things she needed to do, starting with finding a job. Running through the numbers in her head, she knew she was good for at least six months. More if she was exponentially frugal.

She'd amassed a decent savings, and if she watched her spending, she'd be able to pay her bills without pulling out her hair.

She knew of multiple freelance opportunities that she could take advantage of, and most of them were for social media. It would be spare change to help with the bills until something more permanent came along. As she considered all she could do, Stella mused that the timing might have been a blessing in disguise. She had been considering her options for a while, so maybe now was as good a time as any to send out her résumé and writing samples for consideration.

She'd made it to the subway station and stood in the center of the platform waiting for the train. As usual, there was a decent crowd waiting with her. She shifted her box of belongings from one hip to the other, finally resting it on the concrete at her feet as it began to feel heavier and heavier.

A stranger caught her eye, and only because he was staring at her so intensely. He was young and there was something about him that was familiar, but she couldn't put her finger on what it was. She was certain they had never met before but equally sure that it wasn't her first time seeing him. Something about the look he was giving her was off-putting, and she felt her anxiety level rise to an all-time high. He frightened her, and despite the fact she was standing shoulder deep with a crowd surrounding her, she didn't feel safe. She didn't feel safe at all.

Taking a deep breath, she shifted her body so that

she was facing him directly. She tilted her head just so, ensuring he knew she was watching him as hard as he was watching her. His head lifted and his stance straightened. The hint of a smirk pulled at his lips, and he extended his arm to point his index finger at her. At that moment the train pulled into the station, and there was a rush of bodies to get on board. He smiled and took a step forward, and before she gave a second thought to what she doing, Stella lifted her cell phone, engaged the camera and took his picture.

Before he could reach her, she was running to the steps, climbing back out to Forty-Second Street. The box with her possessions was abandoned on the platform, and she hoped someone with the transit department would find it and take it to Lost and Found. As she flagged down a taxi and climbed inside, that man burst onto the sidewalk, looking for her. The smirk on his face had shifted into pure rage. He caught sight of her as the taxi pulled away from the curb. As she stared back at him, Stella could see his anger explode, and he screamed like a wounded animal.

Minutes later, she was safe behind the locked doors of her own home. The alarm was engaged, and she was starting to breathe easier. She sat staring at the photo she'd taken, determined to figure out who that man was. She was drawing a complete blank, and the situation was eerily frustrating. Every few minutes she'd run to the windows to peer outside, but there was nothing there that raised any concerns.

Knowing she'd never be able to find the answers on her own, Stella knew what she'd have to do, and it struck a nerve that didn't sit well with her. But she wasn't left with any other choices.

She dialed Brennan's cell phone. It rang and then went to his voice mail. She hung up and dialed again. On her third try, she left him a message, sharing what had happened. After hanging up, she sent him a text message and attached the photo so that he too had a picture of the man she felt was intent on doing her harm. Glancing out the window one last time, Stella sat and waited, hopeful that Brennan would call her back soon.

The backup on the Triborough Bridge to Queens eastbound along the Grand Central Parkway took longer than anticipated. Just as Brennan's irritation was rising, they made it to the exit at Astoria Boulevard. Bearing left, they headed straight onto 23rd Avenue then left to 82nd Street. A right at the next block, and then another right turn put them exactly at the parking lot of Rikers Island prison.

Rory had called ahead to preregister them for an appointment with Maeve O'Leary, and when they reached the entrance, they were met by a guard. They were relieved of their personal possessions. The contents of their pockets, their cell phones and their government-issued weapons locked away in a courtesy locker.

They traversed the halls to an interrogation room, where they were left to wait for Maeve to be brought down to speak with them. It felt like it was taking forever as the two paced the room from wall to wall.

Minutes later, a guard escorted Maeve O'Leary into the room.

Rory backed her way into the corner, her arms folded around her torso. Brennan stood by the table, waiting patiently as the guard connected her handcuffs and chain to the metal ring secured to the table. With a slight tug of the chain, guaranteeing she was secure, he gave the two of them a nod and exited the room.

"To what do I owe this honor?" Maeve questioned, eyeing Brennan curiously.

Brennan moved to the chair opposite the woman and sat down. Maeve O'Leary was nothing like he expected, despite having seen her image flashed across ever major television network. She was a beautifully stunning woman, tall and slender with delicate features, a warm tan and blonde hair that had been whitewashed by the sun. She was notorious for the many disguises she'd worn to keep herself from being captured by law enforcement.

Maeve was the Black Widow. She was awaiting trial on the murder of her last husband. And the one before him and the one before him and the one before him. Six husbands in all who had fallen for her charms, married her and then had died under mysterious circumstances, leaving her financially wealthier. Maeve was accused of being a serial killer for profit.

"We'd like to ask you some questions," Brennan said after introducing himself and then Rory.

"Questions about what?" Her voice was smooth and rich, like sweet molasses.

Brennan smiled. "You have an admirer. Someone who is killing blond blue-eyed men in their midthirties. The first letter of their first names spells out your name. We were hoping that you might have some idea who that might be."

Maeve laughed. "I was always a good wife. I shouldn't be here. This has been a horrible misunderstanding."

"Your dead husbands might not agree," Rory muttered from her post in the corner.

Maeve never looked in the other woman's direction. Instead, she smiled sweetly and batted her eyelashes at Brennan.

"I'd love to tell you how I met my last husband. Do you have time, Agent Colton?"

Before Brennan could answer, Maeve leaned up on her elbow and began to talk about her life. It would have been entertaining had they nothing else to do and maybe a drink or two to dull the monotony of her stories.

"Really, Maeve," Brennan interrupted. "We're trying to stop anyone else from being hurt. You really need to tell us something."

Maeve smiled sweetly. "Will that pretty girlfriend of yours write about me in that newspaper she works for if I do talk?"

Brennan recoiled, shifting backward too quickly in his chair. "Excuse me?" he snapped, the chair hitting the floor with a dull thud.

"It's the *New York Wire*, isn't it? The newspaper that she works for? I hear tell she's quite the writer.

I'd even consider giving her an exclusive interview if she'd like to come talk to me in person."

Maeve flipped the length of her blonde hair over her shoulder. If she hadn't been wearing the requisite institutional uniform and the shackles around her feet and hands, she would have been a perfect model for a shampoo commercial, Brennan thought.

Rory had moved to his side, her hand resting on his forearm. She didn't speak, and her silence soothed the rising ire that he had wanted to spew. He stepped back as she moved in front of him.

"Mrs. O'Leary, we need to know who you've been talking to. Who's been talking to you about Stella Maxwell? And what do you know about the Landmark Killer cases?"

Maeve waved a dismissive hand at the woman. "It is time for my afternoon constitutional. A girl has to get her beauty rest!"

"Maeve, we need you to answer our questions," Brennan interjected.

"You know what would be nice," Maeve replied. "A down pillow and comforter. Just a few little conveniences from home would make a very nice gift, and very nice gifts might inspire me to tell you what I know."

Brennan shook his head. He knocked on the door and called for the guard. The visit had been total waste of time, because Maeve O'Leary was only interested in self-preservation at any expense.

The guard returned shortly after. "Is there anyone else you need to see, Agent? Detective?"

Brennan shook his head. "No, but we do need to review her visitor logs and any mail she's received."

"I'll need to clear that with the warden first, sir."

"Do whatever you need to do. A man's life is depending on it."

Brennan and Rory returned, having struck out yet again. The prison records didn't get them any closer to discovering who was supplying Maeve with information, and she wasn't talking. But she knew enough to mention Stella. Brennan was still kicking himself for reacting. Had he been playing poker, he would have shown his hand.

As Rory called the rest of the team to update them, Brennan ticked off everything they knew. The list was short and sweet, not a single detail to move the case any further along. It was infuriating, and all of them were frustrated. Having the killer taunt them with details about their family was galling in a way not easily explained. Cash especially fumed over their father's name being bantered about, no respect given to the circumstances of his death and the trauma suffered by his family. Knowing whoever they were looking for possibly worked with them or sat in their inner circle made their situation even more difficult.

"Let it go," Rory said as he pulled up in front of the police station, returning her to her office.

"What do you mean?"

"You need to clear your head. Go home. Watch some television. Read a good book. Do something other than think about this case. Come back to it tomorrow with fresh eyes."

"I wish it was that easy," Brennan said.

"That's an order," Rory stated. "And I get it. I completely understand how you're feeling. But if we're going to win this war, we need to get through the small battles. And we can't do that if we can't focus."

Left with nothing else to say, Brennan waved her away. Before pulling back into traffic, he checked his cell phone. The device was dead.

Chapter 15

Brennan's phone ringing woke him from a deep sleep. He'd been dreaming about the entire team being on an extended vacation to celebrate the trial and conviction of their father's killer. He was just a kid, the age he was when his father had died. His mother was serving freshly baked cookies, and the laughter was thick between them. They were in the old house in Bay Ridge, and they were happy. Happier than they had ever been, right up to the moment the home was surrounded by reporters clamoring for a story. Reporters who were hiding out in the lush bushes, sneaking behind trees with cameras, and jumping out at them from behind parked cars. Reporters calling them by name and asking questions that weren't fun to answer.

It was a bright and cheery dream until it wasn't. And when the phone rang, he was snatched from the first inklings that his dreams were about to become a nightmare.

"Hello?" His voice was low and groggy.

"Are you still asleep?" Sinead questioned.

"I'm not now. What's up?" he said, greeting her warmly. "What time is it?" He squinted his eyes to try and see the clock.

"I need you to stay calm."

"What's going on, Sinead?"

"The *New York Wire* ran a story this morning. It's not pretty. In fact, it's worse than we thought."

Brennan sat upright in his bed. His heart was suddenly racing, and he felt like he'd been punched. "Is it online too?" he asked, catching his breath.

"Yes, I'm sure it is, and Brennan," Sinead hesitated, her nervousness reverberating in her voice.

"Tell me, Sinead."

"It looks like Stella wrote it. Her byline is attached to it."

Brennan cursed, the air punctuated by the harsh vocabulary.

"If you need to call me after your read it, then call. We should all get together later and decide how we want to handle it," Sinead said.

Brennan nodded into the receiver as if she could see him on the other end. "Thanks for calling me," he said.

After disconnecting the line, it took no time at all for Brennan to find the news article. It came with old family photos that had run with the original story when his father had been killed. Pictures of his parents, him and his siblings, and their family home. There were details that only a few were privy to, things he had shared with Stella, trusting they would stay between the two of them. Details she had promised would not be shared. There were also details about the investigation of the Landmark Killer that both the police and FBI had kept to themselves. The story made it seem like the family was acting emotionally, wanting to enact revenge for their father's murder. That those emotions were interfering with them finding the killer. Sinead had been right. It was far worse than he would have ever imagined.

By the time Brennan had showered and dressed, he'd fielded calls from Parker, Ashlyn, Rory, FBI Director Chang and a few close friends. The only person who had not called had been Cashel. Brennan couldn't help but worry about how his twin brother was taking the insult. Having the details of his marriage and divorce play out publicly surely didn't bode well. Stella had violated their trust and attacked their character. She'd made them look foolish, and that was hard to process. His family would need to lean on each other more and consider how this story being out would impact their ability to do their jobs. The Colton family had been attacked, and not one of them was prepared to take that lying down.

Brennan stole one last glance at himself in his bathroom mirror. It would have been different had Stella just came after him. But she had gone after the people he loved most. He had worried how things would play out between the two of them. Now he'd gotten his answer. Stella had shown him her hand, laying all her cards on the table. Sadly, he thought, it was a game that they had both lost.

Stella was enjoying her second cup of coffee that morning when there was a loud pounding on her front door. She hesitated the first time it sounded. The second time, Brennan called her name, screaming at her to open the door.

Moving to the entrance, she was taken aback by his forcefulness. He hadn't returned any of her calls, and she found herself worried that something tragic had happened. Or maybe that stranger was closer to harming her than she'd been ready to believe. Whatever it was, Brennan wasn't happy, which meant she wasn't either.

She snatched the door open and stared at him. "What's going on?"

"Why don't you tell me?" he snapped as he pushed his way past her, moving hurriedly through the entrance.

"How dare you!" Stella snapped back, thrown off guard by the aggression. "I didn't give you permission—"

"And I didn't give you permission either," Brennan said. He held out the early morning edition of the *New York Wire*. "Why, Stella?" he asked. "Just tell me why?"

She snatched the newspaper from his hands and

unfolded it. She inhaled sharply when she saw the headline on the front page.

"Law Enforcement Family Hell-Bent on Revenge." Stella's byline and headshot followed.

Confusion washed over her expression. She gave Brennan a quick glance as she began to read the article. There were photos of him that she had never seen before, details of his father's case and a host of information that she would have never included in any story. Personal information about him and his siblings. It had Brian Price's handiwork all over it.

"Brennan, I didn't do this." She shook her head emphatically.

"Don't lie to me, Stella. After everything that happened between us, please don't lie to me now!" He was shouting, and that unnerved her.

Stella took a step back. "I am not lying. I don't lie. And I would never lie to you. I didn't write this damn story!" she shouted back.

"The *New York Wire* says otherwise."

"I don't care what they say. I don't work for them anymore. I quit yesterday. Brian gave me an ultimatum. This story or you. So I gave them my resignation. I would never have agreed to write something like this. What kind of person do you think I am?"

"Isn't that the million-dollar question? Clearly, you're not the woman I thought you were. I understand you were angry at me, but this article hurt my entire family. Not only did you stab me in the back, but you gutted them as well."

Stella shouted again. "I told you! I did not write

this article! Not one single solitary word! And I didn't give them my permission to credit me for the story. The senior editor has to be behind it. I wouldn't do that to you!"

"You've told me a lot of things, and we see where that got me. And here I was trying to make amends for my own screw-up so we could move forward, and the entire time you were plotting against me."

"I swear to you, Brennan. There is no way I would do something like that to you."

"I don't want to hear it. Clearly, what you were willing to put on paper says otherwise."

"You need to listen to me. We need to fix this."

"Well, you've been right about one thing. There was never any *we* in this relationship. Is this why you were calling me yesterday? To warn me?"

"You didn't read my texts?" Stella's eyes widened, and something like fear washed over her expression.

"No. I deleted you out of my phone. Blocked and deleted! I don't want to see or hear from you ever again."

"Brennan, please!" Stella felt her entire body tense as she pleaded with him. She took a step forward and he backed away.

Brennan moved to the door and stepped back over the threshold. Turning to give her one last look, Brennan shook his head. Tears glazed his eyes. "I can't believe I fell in love with you," he said, his words laced with every ounce of hurt and disappointment he was feeling.

"Brennan!"

"Good-bye, Stella."

* * *

Stepping back inside her home, Stella slammed the door closed. She was still holding that newspaper, and she flung it across the room. What Brian had done was vile, and she would deal with him later. First, though, she had to figure out how to get through to Brennan. He had to know her better than that. She refused to accept that he would think so poorly of her. She understood his hurt, and she knew pain like that would leave anyone angry with the universe.

She also needed help with her stalker problem. If he had not listened to her voice mails or read her text messages, then Brennan didn't know about the man who had chased her. Stella stood ringing her hands together anxiously. If Brennan wouldn't listen, she knew someone else who would. Rushing up the stairs, she hurried to shower and dress. She needed to get to the 130th precinct for help.

When Brennan arrived at the FBI building, Cashel was waiting for him in his office. He and his brother exchanged a look, holding a silent conversation between them. He didn't have to tell Cashel how he was feeling. Cash always knew. Just like he felt it as deeply when something pained his brother.

"Did you talk to Stella?" Cash asked.

"We exchanged words."

"I bet that was entertaining. I would have liked to have been a fly on the wall."

"You didn't miss anything. She insisted she didn't do it. I called her a liar. Now she hates me even more, and I'm still in love with her. But the relationship is over, and we really didn't have a relationship. Hell, we barely knew each other! Then I left before I cried."

"I'm sure that was a sight to behold."

"Lucky for me, I was able to get out of there before I embarrassed myself further."

"Do you really think she did it?" Cash asked, his gaze laser-focused on Brennan's face.

Brennan stared back at his brother. The question wasn't at all what he expected. As he pondered his response, still hesitating, Cash continued.

"I mean, have you really thought about it? This woman meant something to you. So much so that you have been pining for her since things between the two of you went south. You've been making a fool out of yourself over this woman! Would a woman you care that much for do something like this to you?"

"Stella was adamant that she did not write that story. She says her editor at the paper published it and used her name without her permission. In fact, she claims she quit the newspaper yesterday. For that very reason."

"You and I both know anything is possible. People are dirty. We already knew her job was on the line."

"I honestly don't know what to believe. Everything has me on edge. Between her case and the Landmark Killer case, half the time, I don't know if I'm coming or going."

"You have a lot on your plate, which is why you might be reacting without rationalizing."

"I'll be honest with you, Cash. I'm broken right now. Completely broken. Which is why I can't understand how you are managing to be so damn calm. I just knew you'd be ready to break someone's neck."

"Trust and believe, I am not that calm. But something about this just isn't sitting right with me. There were things in that article Stella had no way of knowing. Things I don't believe you would have told her. I'd bet my last dollar that you didn't talk to Stella about my marriage and my divorce. Or that me not wanting kids was an issue.

"Or how our father's death impacted Ashlyn. Or the problems Patrick faced. There were details in that article that only someone with personal knowledge of each of us would have. Or that someone with access would find in our personnel files. Things that would have come out during our required psychological evaluations."

Brennan's head snapped up as he and Cash locked eyes. "Stella said that email the other day about those anonymous text messages that Sinead and I received set off the newspaper wanting to do an article."

Cash nodded. "And is it possible that whoever sent that message didn't also feed more information to someone else there?"

"I really think we need to pay her editor a visit."

"Is this visit on the record or off?" Cash queried, a slow smile pulling across his face.

"Oh, this is definitely off the record. And it won't be FBI-sanctioned either."

Stella hesitated at the top of her steps. She looked left down the block and then right. It was relatively quiet for the midmorning hour, not much activity stirring things up. She had called and left a message for Detective Rory Colton, but she hadn't called her back yet. She couldn't help but wonder if the entire family was furious with her, believing she had betrayed them.

She'd left a message with an Officer Davis, wanting Rory to know that she was headed in that direction. She didn't add that she was scared, but deep down inside, Stella was petrified. She was still debating whether to call for an Uber or take the subway. She hated that she was starting to feel like a hostage in her own skin. And it infuriated her that some nameless, faceless person had that much control over her life.

She took a deep breath, her decision made. Easing down the steps, Stella lifted her head, her chin high up. Pulling her shoulders back, she took one more deep breath and began to walk toward the subway station.

The two brothers walking into the offices of the *New York Wire* looked like movie gold. They seemed bigger than life: tall, handsome and determined. As they glided by, people paused at the sight of them. Their jawlines were set like stone, and the look in their eyes was pure fury.

Brian Price's eyes widened nervously as they stormed into his office unannounced. He'd been sitting back with his hands clasped behind his head and his feet up on the desk. He'd been thinking how well his day had started, watching the growing website numbers. People were weighing in with their opinions on the front-page story about the Colton family. To suddenly have two of the brothers standing in front of him was disconcerting.

"You don't have an appointment," he stammered, looking from one to the other.

Brennan moved to the man's left side and Cash eased over to his right. Brennan sat down on the desktop, nudging Brian's legs to the floor.

"What do you want?"

"We need to speak with Ms. Maxwell about her story this morning," Brennan said. "Is she in yet?"

Brian cleared his throat. "I can't have you trying to intimidate my reporters."

"Will she feel intimidated?" Cash asked.

"I feel intimidated. You have no right to try and strong-arm me."

Brennan smiled. "That's not at all what we're doing. We just have some questions. We're going to give her the opportunity to answer them here. Now. Or in court, when we sue."

Brian coughed. "I'm sure every fact was checked and verified."

"Are you sure about that?" Cash asked.

"Why don't you call her in so that we can verify that? She did write the article, didn't she?" Brennan asked.

Brian stammered again. "I…we…she's not…"

"What, Brian? Spit it out!" Brennan said, his voice raised slightly.

"Who supplied you with the information?" Cash interjected.

"I can't reveal my source!"

"You can't? Wasn't Stella your source?"

"Her source…" he muttered.

"We passed Ms. Maxwell's desk on the way in, and it was empty. That doesn't look good, Brian. It looks like she quit or was fired. Which is it?"

"She…we…it's not…"

"You write so creatively. I'm surprised you're having a hard time getting your words out."

"This is unacceptable," Brian shouted.

Brennan leaned back, humming contemplatively. "I sure hope she still works here, Brian. And that you can verify it. If not…"

Cash leaned in and whispered into the man's ear. "In the business, we call that identity theft."

"Fifteen years max, with heavy fines if the victim faced financial losses," Brennan continued. "Legal fees, perhaps."

Brian's eyes darted between the two men. "You're bluffing."

Cash shrugged. "Alternatively, you could clear this up now and give us your sources. What's it going to be?"

Brian was not at all happy about his current situation. He pointed to the bottom drawer of his desk. Cash pulled it open and pulled out a large manila folder that rested on top. The Colton name had been neatly typed on the side tab.

"Get out of my office," Brian snapped. "That's everything I have."

"*Did* Stella Maxwell write that story?" Brennan asked.

Brian didn't voice the answer out loud, only glared. That was all the confirmation Brennan needed.

"Pleasure doing business with you," Cash called back cheerfully.

"I'll be filing a complaint with your superiors!" Brian shouted.

Brennan paused in the doorway. "You do that. We look forward to it. Have a good day now!"

The duo returned to the elevator and waited for it to reach their floor. Brennan smiled. She didn't write the article. Now all he needed to do was to find Stella and grovel for forgiveness.

Chapter 16

Stella was just six short blocks from the police station when she saw the man from the previous day. He stood on the other side of the street dressed in a black hoodie and matching sweatpants. He stood out because the day's temperature was pushing ninety degrees, and he was dressed for a winter snowstorm. There were enough people on the street that she didn't feel like she'd be an easy target, but then she thought about her delivery man and the police officer. They hadn't seen her as an easy target either, not knowing that they were directly in the line of fire. Stella would have been devastated if one more person was caught in the cross-fire of someone trying to get to her.

She came to an abrupt halt as she weighed her options. He was smoking a cigarette, leaning against the wall of an office building. They traded gazes as he seemed to be waiting for her next move. Which is why she stood still, her feet frozen to the sidewalk as she in turn waited for him. She refused to show him any fear. If he was coming for her, she fully intended to give him one hell of a fight. She prayed that the expression on her face showed him that.

She watched as he took a step forward. He dropped the cigarette butt to the ground and smashed it beneath the heavy steel-toed boots he wore. His gaze moved down the block, and he stared before turning back to give her a smug glare.

She shifted her gaze to where he had looked, and her breath caught in her chest. Crossing the intersection was another man who looked identical to the guy across the street. He too was dressed all in black with a hoodie on. Twins, she thought, the reality of her situation beginning to take hold. Not one potential villain out to get her but two. Suddenly both men were headed in her direction.

Stella turned, moving forward. She had just reached the corner and was crossing the street when she caught sight of the third man. *Triplets?* She suddenly felt outnumbered, and the police precinct was still five blocks away.

A horn blowing drew her attention, and when she looked over, a GOP campaign truck was pulling up to the curb. The outside had been repainted with the image of the new candidate, Marshall Tucker for Governor, in bold black print. Pamela sat behind the wheel, waving at Stella excitedly.

Grateful for the bright smile shining on her, Stella glanced behind her and rushed toward the idling vehicle. She jumped into the passenger seat, slamming the door shut and locking it behind her.

When she turned toward Pamela, the other woman was still grinning excitedly.

"Everything okay?" Pamela questioned as she pulled back into traffic.

Stella glanced back at the trio of ninja-suited strangers. They were standing together, staring after the van. Stella eyed them through the side view mirror, her gaze frozen in place until they were out of sight.

Sitting back in the seat, she breathed a sigh of relief. "Thank you. I'm good now."

She turned back to Pamela whose smile had waned substantially. It was that very moment when Stella realized the mistake she had made. The man from the previous day had seemed familiar, and she now saw the resemblance as if someone had painted the picture for her. It was their eyes. Pamela and the stranger had the same eyes.

Stella feigned a smile and pointed out the passenger side window. "If you can just drop me off around the corner here. I have an appointment with the detective on Rockwell's case. She's expecting me."

Pamela shook her head as she made a left turn at the light, heading in the opposite direction. "I don't think that's a good idea, Stella," Pamela said, losing the cheery tone to her voice. "I think you and I really need to talk."

"Really, Pamela. This is important, and I don't

have time for your games!" There was a nervous edge to Stella's voice, the sound foreign to her own ears. She turned back to give the other woman a look, and that's when she realized Pamela was pointing a gun right at her.

"Stella didn't write that article!" Brennan exclaimed as he entered the conference room at FBI headquarters.

The team had all gathered to discuss what had happened and update each other on anything they might have learned. He moved to the seat at the end of the table.

All eyes turned to give him a look. Amusement wafted from one to the other.

Patrick spoke first. "You seem especially excited about that."

Ashlyn nodded. "Almost giddy. Like you'd actually believed she'd done it before."

Brennan shrugged. "I had concerns."

His sister turned to Sinead. "Why are men such asswipes?"

Sinead laughed. "I can't answer that. My man is a gem."

"So, who wrote the story?" Patrick asked.

Cash answered the question. "Stella's boss. Our mole fed him information about all of us. Practically told him the story he should write. He gave us his documents, and based on what he had, we were able to get a warrant for his computers. The digital forensics team is examining them as we speak."

Patrick gave him a high five. "Good job!"

The conference room door suddenly swung open. Rory, Wells and Director Chang moved into the space. Rory shot the twin brothers a look. Wells eyed them also, rolling his eyes skyward. The director's glare was edged in criticism, and the entire team could feel a reprimand coming. Rory took the seat beside Brennan and kicked him under the table.

Detective Chang was tall and exceptionally lean. Her straight black hair was in a short pixie cut that complemented her dark eyes. She wore silver-framed glasses and a black silk suit that hugged her petite frame. Her expression was serious, and she was known for being straight-forward and painfully direct.

The room went quiet as she eyed them one by one, her stare pausing on Brennan and then shifting to Cash. "Can someone please explain to me why I've spent the last hour fielding a civilian complaint about two of my agents harassing a newspaper editor?"

"We did no such thing," Cash said.

Brennan nodded. "We were asking him about information he'd received, and gave him some friendly legal advice. Then we left."

Detective Chang shook her head. "I'll need written statements from you both," she said. "And there's to be no further contact between you two and anyone at the *New York Wire*. Is that understood?"

"Yes, ma'am," Brennan said.

"Where are we with the Landmark Killer case?" she asked.

For the next hour the team updated the director on all they'd been able to accomplish and where they were still hitting a brick wall. She reiterated the importance of them closing the case as quickly as possible. Reminding them the mayor was breathing down her neck, and she would continue to put pressure on them when he was making her life miserable.

When the conversation was finished, the director looked at her watch. "I have a plane to catch. If any of you need me, Xander will know where to find me."

A chorus of appreciation and well wishes rang through the room.

"Thank you, Director," Brennan said.

"Safe travels," Cash interjected.

When the door closed after her, the two blew sighs of relief. Laughter rang warmly through the room.

"I can't believe you two," Ashlyn said.

"Believe it," Rory countered. "The fool editor has been on the rampage for most of the afternoon. He wasn't happy with the two of you."

"He's pond scum," Brennan said. "What little attention he deserved from us is done and finished. He just wants another fifteen minutes to redeem himself for being an idiot."

"There's no saving idiots," Cash said matter-of-factly.

Parker rose from his seat. "I'm headed down to forensics. I'll call you once I see if they're getting anywhere."

"Thanks," Brennan said.

Rory was listening to her cell phone. Her expression changed, the easy glow shifting to something dark and serious. She held up her hand, moving them all to quiet down as she jotted notes onto the notepad before her. When she was finished, she paused to text a message, promptly hitting the Send button when she was done.

"Have you heard from Stella?" she asked turning to give Brennan a look.

He shook his head. "Not since I spoke to her this morning. It was before I learned the truth, and I was angry."

"Check your messages. She said she sent something to you yesterday."

Brennan suddenly looked contrite. "She told me that too. I lied and told her I had blocked and deleted her and her messages. The truth was my phone died and I hadn't had a chance to review them."

Rory shook her head. "Well, you being an idiot may well have just gotten her killed," she said, rising swiftly from her seat. She played the voice mail on her phone, putting the device on speaker. Stella's voice came through clearly.

"Detective Colton? Rory? This is Stella. I really need help. I'm sending you a photo of a man who came after me yesterday in the subway. He'd been watching me, and he chased me out. I think it might be the man you're looking for. The man who killed Rockwell. He's familiar to me, but I don't know where I recognize him from. I've tried to reach Brennan, but he's not answering me. He's mad at me. But I'm mad at him too, so we really are of no use to each other.

I've sent him the photo also. I'm headed to the precinct now. I should be there within the hour."

Rory tossed Brennan a look. "That was four hours ago. Check your messages!"

Brennan picked up his phone. There was a single missed call and voice mail from Stella. He put the phone on speaker and pushed the Play button. There were two voices, and both were muffled, but there was no mistaking that it was Stella in conversation with someone. Somehow, Stella had managed to hit the redial button on the last call she had placed.

"Stop talking!" a woman was saying, exasperation filling her tone.

"You need to let me go. You don't need to do this."

"Don't tell me what I need to do."

"Then just explain it to me. Help me understand why. Why did you kill Rockwell?"

The woman laughed. A deep bone-chilling chortle that made the hairs rise on Brennan's neck.

Stella persisted. "Why did you do it? And the bomb? What were you thinking?"

"Make her stop talking!" the woman shouted. "I have to think!"

Stella suddenly cried out, her scream cut short as if she were suddenly choking. And just like that, there was silence.

Brennan pushed the Stop button and began to scroll through the text messages that Stella had sent the day before. His eyes widened as he read them. Then he saw the photo, and he too had a sense of familiarity that he found unsettling. He was squinting as he tried to make the image larger on the screen.

Ashlyn snatched the phone from her brother's hands. "I'll be right back. I'll get this enlarged and printed out."

Brennan nodded. He'd gone cold, his blood feeling like ice water pumping through his heart. He'd been angry and had gotten so caught up with finding out the truth about that damn article that he'd forgotten about her messages. He'd screwed up royally, and now Stella was in serious trouble. He didn't know if he'd be able to recover if he failed her again. He suddenly felt helpless, and he had no doubts that it showed on his face.

"We'll plug into all the city cameras between her house and the precinct to see if we can find her," Parker said, racing from the room.

"Her phone's off," Rory said, trying to call her. "I've got my guys tracing the last cell tower it pinged."

"Grab your files," Cash said, his tone calm. "Let's go through everything you have to see what we might have missed."

"I've gone through them a million times," Brennan muttered.

"You haven't reviewed the last one I tossed onto your desk. My office only left it there this morning, and we took off shortly after."

"What file is that?"

"You requested everything I could find on that campaign woman."

Brennan nodded just as Ashlyn moved back into

the room. She'd enlarged the photograph, capturing a clear image of a young man wearing sweats. He was smirking, the look he was giving the camera feeling like it could burn a hole in concrete.

"We're running it through facial recognition software right now," his sister said.

Brennan was staring at the image, his mind on overload as it worked like an unhinged computer. Why was that face familiar? Where had he seen that man before? It was beginning to drive him crazy, most especially because his remembering could be the answer to finding Stella.

When he looked up, Cash and Sinead had split up the files on Stella's case and were beginning to go through them. His brother pushed the folder labeled with Pamela Littlefield's name across the table toward him. And then it clicked.

Grabbing the image of Pamela Littlefield and the photo of their unidentified perp, he held them both up, side by side. He looked from one to the other, back and forth. The resemblance was undeniable. It was deeply embedded in their eyes, their gazes identical, his equally as beautiful as hers.

Chapter 17

"Pamela Littlefield was a quadruplet, the only girl and the eldest in the set of four. Parents were Leona and Eddie Littlefield. Mom died during childbirth. Pamela was delivered safely, but complications left the three boys compromised. They were deprived of oxygen and suffered maturation deficits after birth. According to the report, that part of the brain that controlled speech was affected, and none of the boys has ever spoken. It was believed that they were mentally challenged, and they were committed to a home care facility at a young age where treatment and care meant handcuffing them to beds and locking them in cages. Pamela was raised by her father until his death when she was sixteen. At the age of nineteen, she petitioned for guardianship of her brothers and won."

Sinead looked up from the document she'd been reading. Her expression was telling.

"What?" Brennan questioned. "What does it say?"

"The father died in a house fire. They weren't able to prove it, but Pamela was suspected of starting that fire."

"Well, that wasn't her last rodeo," Cash said. "That was not the only person murdered where Pamela was a suspect. And the brothers have lengthy criminal records. But she always manages to get them all cleared. It seems her political connections have come in handy." He passed a document to his brother, who read it and passed it back.

"It's been her the whole time," Brennan said. "And her brothers have been helping her."

Silence swept through the room. Without saying it out loud, they were all thinking the same thing. Stella was in serious trouble.

Stella had no idea where she was. She believed they were somewhere in the South Bronx, remembering them exiting off the Bruckner Expressway toward Hunts Point. Pamela had driven the truck through bay doors, coming to a stop inside a warehouse. From what she'd been able to ascertain, the warehouse was home for Pamela's brothers.

She shook her head. Pamela had introduced her family as if she expected them and Stella to become fast friends. Owen, Charlie and Miles had only stared at her as if she were an albatross they couldn't wait to be rid of. They weren't happy about her being in their space, and Pamela seemed completely oblivious to that fact.

Pamela was off in her own little bubble, narrowly focused on the problem that was Stella. Trying to figure out how to eliminate Stella and get away with it.

From where they had forced her to sit, Stella had a front-row view of the room and the family. One of the brothers, the one named Owen, Stella thought, was hunched over a table, playing with wires and boxes and batteries. Every so often, he would chuckle, seemingly pleased with whatever he was working on.

The brother named Miles was with Pamela, seemingly distressed over something. He sat cradled against Pamela's lap as she stroked his back and rocked him back and forth. Charlie had disappeared, nowhere to be found. Not knowing when he might pop up or where didn't give Stella any comfort whatsoever.

They had found her cell phone, turning off the device and throwing into a trash dumpster blocks away. She wasn't confident that her last calls had gotten through. Whether or not Brennan or any of his team would come for her felt unlikely. She was alone, and if she were going to survive this, she would need to remain calm.

Pamela suddenly rose from her seat. She was yelling at Miles and then she slapped him. Hard. He reacted violently, sending everything atop a desk in the room to the floor. Pamela stood with her hands on her hips, chastising him until he finally calmed down.

At least an hour passed by before Pamela shifted

her attention back to Stella. She marched across the room, halting abruptly in front of her.

"Are you hungry?" Pamela asked. She gave Stella a bright smile. "I can send one of the boys to pick you something up. Any requests for your last meal?" She laughed as if that were funny.

Stella shook her head. "No. Thank you."

"Suit yourself," Pamela said. She turned to cross back to where she'd been earlier.

Stella called after her. "Pamela, please tell me why you're doing this. Please!"

Pamela smiled. "Because I can!"

"Why did you kill Rockwell?"

"To make the world a better place, of course!" Her expression was stunned, as if she couldn't fathom Stella not making sense of it all. "Rockwell wasn't' always a nice man. You know that."

"I don't understand. You and Rockwell were friends."

"No, we weren't. Rockwell's mother was his only friend."

"But why set me up to take the fall?"

"You were supposed to die too. It was supposed to be a murder-suicide, but Miles messed up. He sent you the message too soon. If he had waited, I'd have been able to slit your throat and leave you for dead beside Rockwell. And it had to be you. It just made sense. Your fingerprints on the knife would have sealed the deal!"

"How did you do that?" Stella questioned. "Put my fingerprints on the murder weapon?"

Pamela jumped excitedly. "We saw it on television one night. On that show Matlock! It was so cool. You take a piece of clear tape and press it down over an original fingerprint. Then you transfer the print to another item. I got the knife from Rockwell's kitchen that night we were all there for pizza. And I lifted the fingerprint from your water bottle after you and Rockwell left me to clean up. He had walked you to the subway station. As soon as you got on the train, he went to meet Rebecca. She wanted to reconcile, and I think he did too, but you were in the way, always being pushy with his time. His mother said you were a problem, and I'm good at getting rid of problems."

"But his mother didn't want Rockwell dead. That doesn't make any sense!" Confusion washed over Stella's expression.

"It makes sense because that's how we wanted to play the game. We decide who lives and who dies. We decide how and when. We always make sure whoever is supposed to be guilty, looks guilty. Always! This would have worked if we had killed you both in your house like I suggested, but it was one of the boys that wanted to see if we could pull it off in broad daylight. But he got the timing wrong, and now I have to clean up the mess."

"You've done this before?"

"Of course, silly!"

"Why the bomb?"

"The boys again!" Pamela said, her singsong tone irritating. "Owen tried to make things right. But you got away again! Now I have to do it. Charlie wanted a turn, but he tends to be messy. And messy makes law enforcement want to figure out what happened. Charlie would have tried when you were in the hospital, but he could never get past that cute Agent Colton. So now it's my turn. Your dead body floating in the Harlem River can look like an accident. Or a suicide. No mess. No blame. Game over."

"You're going to get caught. The Coltons are going to figure this out."

Pamela's tone was saccharine sweet and condescending. "You want to believe that. I understand. And that's okay. But I know, you're going to die, and then I'm going to a fundraiser for our new candidate. And tomorrow, my brothers and I will pick someone new to play with!"

Brennan stole away to his office, closing and locking the door behind him. His head throbbed, and his heart felt like it might burst out of his chest. He knew he needed to step back and calm down before he gave himself a stroke or a heart attack.

They'd been searching for Stella for most of the afternoon. It was as if she'd disappeared off the face of the earth. A patrol car had been parked back in front of her home, and he'd gone there himself to check that she wasn't lying hurt or dead inside. The team had pulled together to help search for her and the Littlefield family, who were all looking like serial killers who had flown so far under the radar that no one would have ever considered them suspect.

Sinead had attributed at least twelve murders to

their handiwork, with twenty other unsolved crimes she liked them for. The more that was discovered about them, the more fire they were able to throw on a host of cold cases. But Brennan couldn't focus on what they had possibly done in the past. He was only concerned with what they might do in the future. What harm they might bring to Stella if he couldn't find her soon.

Tobias and the Henleys had been brought in for questioning. The Henleys couldn't fathom Pamela being able to do such a thing. Mrs. Henley had accused him of grasping at straws to make a case. That he was making everyone a suspect because he wasn't good at doing his job. She earnestly believed that Pamela could never do Rockwell any harm. Discovering that Pamela had three brothers had stalled any further comments, the couple admitting that maybe they didn't know the young woman as well as they thought they did.

Tobias knew the family's history. He acknowledged the brothers had always been problematic, but rarely did he see them. According to him, Pamela never talked about her siblings at all. Unless, of course, she needed help to keep one of them out of jail. He didn't seem at all surprised to hear that she was suspected in Rockwell's death. Brennan found that strange. When he asked Tobias if he had ever been concerned about Pamela working for him, he'd been dismissive, believing that as long as she needed him, he was good to go. Tobias had been asked if he had any idea where Stella could be found, and he had denied any knowledge of her whereabouts. Brennan found that hard to believe. When he considered the time Pamela spent lost up her employer's backside, following him around, nothing Tobias said sounded reasonable.

He remembered Stella thinking Pamela might have been in love with Tobias, and he had asked him about that as well. He'd responded with a dismissive shrug and a wry smile, like Pamela was one of many women who fawned all over him.

The Henleys and Tobias had shared as much information as possible before being escorted back to their homes.

Before retreating to his office, Brennan had left his sister and cousin to follow up on the leads they'd been given. Each of them was putting in extra hours to get things done. He didn't have words to express how much their efforts meant to him. Finding Stella was going to take all the manpower they could muster, and doing it all on his own was never an option.

Brennan pulled open the bottom drawer of his desk. He pulled a bottle of bourbon and a small shot glass from inside. He poured himself a quick drink and downed it without blinking an eye. For ten more minutes he sat inhaling and exhaling deep cleansing breaths. When he began to feel more like himself, he stood up and stretched. Deep down in his midsection his gut instincts had kicked into high gear, and there would be no ignoring them.

Brennan hurried back to the conference room that had become serial killer central. He rushed through the door shouting orders. "Let's do a deeper dive on Tobias. Something tells me his connection to Pamela isn't as casual as he would like us to believe."

Stella couldn't believe she'd actually dozed off to sleep. She woke with a start, unsettled as she remembered where she was and why. She had no clue how long she'd been there or what the others had been up to. As her eyes adjusted to the dim light, she jumped, fright spiraling up and down the length of her spine.

One of the brothers was sitting in front of her, watching her closely. His head tilted slightly to the side and his eyes widened when he realized she was awake. Stella made herself smile, unsure what he was doing or why. He just stared, his body down in a low squat.

"Hi," she said, her voice low. "You're Charlie, right?"

He didn't answer, only shifted his head to the other side as he kept staring.

Stella tried again to engage him in conversation, but she got nothing. As she thought about it, she hadn't heard one of them speak. Not a single word since she'd been taken. Pamela had been their voice, telling them what the other was saying. They didn't sign, nor had she seen either of them write a note to communicate. Pamela seemed to be their only link to each other and the outside world.

As if the devil had heard her thoughts, Pamela called her brother's name. "Charlie! What are you doing? Get away from her! It's not time yet."

Charlie began to rock back and forth. When Pamela called him a second time, moving in their direction, he stood up straight and rushed past her, dodging a blow as she swung a fist in the direction of his head.

Pamela stood where Charlie had just been resting. "Have you no shame?" she snapped at Stella, a look of disgust on her face.

Stella glared up at her. "I just said hello to him."

"I see how you flirt. You always need to be the center of attention. That's why I picked you. Charlie didn't want you to get tagged for the game. That's only because you have him snowed too. Like you did Rockwell."

"You are seriously delusional."

Pamela bristled, but she didn't respond.

"Why don't they talk?" Stella asked. "I haven't heard your brothers speak."

"They talk. They talk to me and they talk to God. They don't need to talk to you or anyone else. It's our gift. We were blessed with it when we were all together in our mother's womb. It's why we're special. We've been chosen for great things. I hear all their thoughts. They don't need words for me to know what they want to say."

Stella shook her head and muttered under her breath. "Like I said, delusional!"

Pamela screamed, the sound like nails on a chalkboard. Stella's eyes widened, her heartbeat beginning to race. She shifted back against the wall, sliding closer to the corner. Pamela continued to scream, seeming to unleash whatever emotion she might have been feeling. Behind her, the brothers barely blinked, their sister's tantrum not even registering an ounce of emotion from them. Stella shook her head.

"What are you going to do with me?" she asked as Pamela finally paused to take a breath.

Pamela smiled, collecting herself as if nothing had happened. "I'm not going to do anything to you. You are going to overdose on pain medication and fall into the Harlem River. You've been distraught over being accused of killing Rockwell and then having someone trying to kill you. It was more than you could take. I told you, Stella. We have to make the details fit the story!"

Stella pulled at the zip ties that secured her hands and tied one ankle to a steel rod that ran from floor to ceiling. She been trying to work herself free when she thought no one was looking, but soon discovered one or more of them were always looking. Pamela had slapped her the last time, something like rage gleaning through her fingers and palm.

Time seemed to be standing still, and Stella was grateful for it. Pamela appeared to have her own schedule of doing things, and she would not be moved from Stella dying at precisely the right time. That had bought her an extra hour or two for Brennan to figure out where she was so he could come save her.

Stella had all the faith in the world that Brennan Colton would save her. She imagined him and his team working to put all the puzzle pieces together until they exposed the criminals from everyone else.

He would work things out, and those details Pamela was so proud of would inevitably be her downfall. At least, that's what Stella was praying for.

She missed him. She would have given up a first-born son, the family cow if they'd had one and even an appendage to be able to press herself against him one more time. She wanted to feel him so close that it would be like they were conjoined twins. She wanted to apologize for pushing him away. She needed to make things right between them. She had salvaged rage that was not his and had tried to drown him with it. She'd not given him a second chance, and that had come from dating way too many men who hadn't deserved one. She prayed that there would still be time for her to make things right. Because all she wanted to do was to tell Brennan that she loved him.

Chapter 18

"Bingo!" Ashlyn jumped from her seat. She rushed to the printer and pulled a stack of papers from the receptacle tray. She waved them high in the air for everyone's attention. "Tobias Humphrey was born Tobias Tyson Hodges. Legally changed his name ten years ago after graduating from community college in New Jersey. In his high school yearbook, he was voted the student most likely to succeed. I bet you can't guess who his prom date was, and your first two choices don't count."

"I'll do you one better," Sinead interjected. "At least six of the deaths we believe the family is responsible for are individuals with connections to one Tobias Humphrey. It was believed the last couple died in a home invasion gone wrong. The husband was campaign manager for an opposing candidate. Another victim was a college professor who gave him a failing grade. It looks like they were eliminating people Tobias had problems with."

"And that's why they targeted Rockwell and Stella!" Brennan exclaimed. "She wasn't making things easy, and Rockwell had continued to support her. Getting rid of them both allowed Tobias to start over."

Everyone was nodding. "And didn't I see something in your notes about her having a boyfriend named Tyson?" Rory asked. "Tobias and Tyson are one and the same!"

"Where would they take Stella?" Brennan questioned. "Did we get anything on the city's camera feeds?"

"This is so your lucky day!" Patrick chimed. "A campaign van was seen in the vicinity of police headquarter around the time Stella made those calls. We were able to track it to Queens. And for the topping on that cake, her phone has been pinging off a cell tower that's close to the last camera sighting. And I can unofficially say those calls are coming from Tobias's phone."

"Why unofficially?" Ashlyn asked.

"Because it's not information we're supposed to have without the appropriate warrants. But I have friends!"

"What's in Queens?" Brennan asked.

"We're still looking. We're searching public records to see if Pamela owned any property or is connected to any business there."

"Let's add Tobias to that search as well."

Rory rose from her seat and gestured in Brennan's direction. "There's a fancy campaign fundraiser tonight. I say we take this show on the road and go pay Ms. Littlefield a visit."

Wells suddenly moved toward the door, pushing buttons on his cell phone before he reached the entrance. "I'm calling the district attorney. We're going to need warrants for both their homes, campaign headquarters, all cell phones, and you're going to need warrants for their arrest. I've also put out an all-points bulletin for Stella Maxwell. We'll find her!"

Brennan nodded, giving Rory a look. "Let's dance, Detective Colton!"

Pamela and one of her brothers were dancing a bossa nova toward Stella. Or rather, Pamela was dancing and pulling the man along with her. She had changed and was now wearing a floor-length gown in a vibrant shade of emerald.

"Don't you look nice," Stella said casually. Her stare was suspicious.

"Thank you. My fiancé picked it out. Tyson loves this color on me, and he says we need to make a grand appearance at tonight's fundraiser."

"Will he be joining you here?" Stella asked.

Pamela stared at her, and then she laughed. "He doesn't need to join me here. I'll be going to him. But good try, Stella Maxwell!"

"You need to let me go, Pamela. We can fix this."

"It's already been fixed. Unfortunately, I have to shift to plan B. That boyfriend of yours has gotten too close, and Tyson says we need to cut our losses while we can still get out of this." She pressed a hand over her bosom. "It hurts my heart too! But we always knew this day might come."

"I don't understand," Stella said, confusion teasing her expression.

The dress Pamela wore had pockets, and she suddenly pulled a cell phone from inside. She read the screen and then she shook her head. "The things we will do for the men we love!" She turned, walking back to the other side of the oversized room and small office against the front wall.

Stella watched as the brothers followed her inside. Pamela wrapped each one in a warm embrace before kissing their cheeks. They retreated to their respective corners, the simple good-bye seemingly an innocent display of affection.

Pamela moved back to her. She carried a small bottle of water in her hand. Charlie followed on her heels, and when they reached Stella's side, he squatted down next to her. Pamela smiled that bright smile of hers.

"Share your candy with Stella," Pamela said.

Charlie opened his hands to show Stella the small white pills inside his palms. He suddenly shoved a handful into Stella's mouth, forcing her to swallow them. Stella gagged, feeling like she might choke as they slid down her throat, and then she coughed, spitting the taste of them out of her mouth. "What the hell did you just give me?" she snapped.

Charlie had swallowed his pills and was drinking

the last of that bottled water. He began to rock back and forth, his eyes closed.

Pamela knelt down to kiss his forehead. "It won't be long now, Stella," she said softly. "You'll just drift off to sleep and everything will be glorious! See," she said as she pointed toward the other two brothers.

Owen sat in a recliner in front of a small television. He'd fallen to his side as if he'd drifted off to sleep. Miles sat at his worktable, his movements unsteady, until he too slipped down to the floor.

Stella felt a layer of fog descending across her brain. Her eyelids had gone heavy, and she struggled to keep them open. "What...what...did you give us?" she stammered, her voice barely a whisper.

"It doesn't matter," Pamela said. "I just needed to make quick work of the cleanup."

"They'll...they'll find us," Stella said, her whole body feeling as if every muscle had suddenly gone limp.

"They will," Pamela said. "Maybe months from now. I doubt there'll be anything left of you though, except maybe your bones. I don't think the rats eat the bones." She genuinely looked confused as she considered her own statement. "Just sleep, Stella. Don't fight it. Just sleep and you won't even know when it happens."

Charlie had curled himself against Stella's side. A single tear rained out of his eyes and down his cheek. Stella leaned over him, no understanding of how Pamela could harm her family. She closed her own eyes and felt her breathing begin to labor. Everything around her went quiet. In the distance, Pamela was humming to herself, and then the roar of a truck engine echoed out of the bay door. Pamela had left them there to die.

The campaign fundraiser for the new candidate was being held at New York's Helen Mills. The venue was a stunning four-thousand-square-foot space with a beautiful thirty-seven-foot-long hand-crafted bar and a multiseat theater. Some three hundred people had been invited for a cocktail-style reception.

Brennan and Rory entered the venue followed by a team of ten NYPD uniformed officers. He held the arrest warrants in his hand and eagerly searched out Tobias and Pamela. He found them huddled together in a corner, Tobias looking upset by something. Pamela caught sight of them first, and she waved them over, the exuberant gesture unsettling.

"Special Agent Colton, to what do we owe this honor?" Pamela said, her tone too cheery. "Have you come to endorse our candidate?"

"Where's Stella Maxwell?" Brennan said, firing the question at her. "And your brothers? Where have they taken her?"

Pamela looked confused. "Stella? I haven't seen Stella in ages. And what does this have to do with my brothers?" She cut an eye toward Tobias.

Tobias took a protective step in front of the woman. "What is this about, Agent? Why are you and the detective here?"

"You're both wanted for questioning in the disappearance of Stella Maxwell, as well as multiple un-solved murders here in Manhattan," Rory said. She took a step behind Pamela. "Put your hands behind your back," she said.

"This is ridiculous!" Pamela exclaimed.

"If you want to make this difficult, you can try," Rory said. "But it will not end well for you."

Two of the uniformed officers stepped forward, their hands perched precariously on their guns.

Pamela gave them that gummy smile. "Now why would I be difficult? I'm sure this is a simple mis-understanding." She pulled both arms to her back side, flinching ever so slightly when those handcuffs clicked and locked.

"You have the right to remain silent. Anything you say can and will be used against you in a court of law…" Rory began to Mirandize the woman.

Brennan had already snapped handcuffs on Tobias, and he did the same. "…You have the right to an at-torney. If you cannot afford an attorney, one will be provided to you. Do you understand the rights I have just read to you?"

Tobias nodded, his eyes rolling skyward as if he were annoyed and bored.

"This is just so unnecessary," Pamela quipped.

"With these rights in mind, do you wish to speak with me?" Brennan questioned. "Are you ready to tell me where I can find Stella Maxwell?"

Tobias chuckled. He answered, "I'd like to speak with my attorney."

Pamela shook her head. "So sad that she would suddenly disappear like that."

Tobias repeated himself a second time, staring directly at Pamela in a silent conversation meant only for her. "Attorney!"

Brennan was watching as Tobias and Pamela were placed in the back of two patrol cars headed to the precinct for processing and questioning. Although there was a level of satisfaction knowing they'd just gotten two serial killers off the streets, his anxiety over not knowing where Stella could be was at an all-time high. He desperately needed to find her. And he needed to find her safe and well.

Rory moved out of the building onto the sidewalk. She tossed Brennan a look, seeming to understand what he hadn't verbalized. He nodded his head and gave her a slight smile.

"You good?" Brennan asked.

She nodded. "I'm good. I'm headed to the station to get them processed."

"Don't let the bobo twins interrogate them, please?"

Rory laughed. "The bobo twins?"

"Those two you let interrogate Stella. Frick and Frack. We don't need to lose this case on their stupidity. And those two," he pointed at Tobias and Pamela. "Those two are cunning! With them already lawyering up, we'll have an uphill battle to bring them to justice."

"Rest assured, only Wells and I will be interrogating them. This is way too big for any of us to be messing it up." She pressed her hand to his back as she eased past him, heading to her own ride. Watching his cousin walk away, Brennan felt assured that whatever else followed would be a walk in the park.

The cell phone in his pocket vibrated for his attention. He didn't need to look at the screen to know it was his brother calling, the ringtone designated specifically for him.

"What's up?" Brennan answered.

Cash didn't hesitate to reply. "We found Stella. I've texted you the address."

Chapter 19

Brennan barreled toward Hunt's Point in the South Bronx with his sirens blaring. He exited the Bruckner Expressway, running parallel with the Bronx River. Property tax records showed an old warehouse near the food distribution center owned by Tobias Tyson Hodges. Cash had taken an FBI tactical team to investigate the premises and had found Stella restrained inside. His brother hadn't said she was okay, so Brennan was desperately trying to prepare himself for the worst.

As he pulled into the lot, FBI agents and local police were spread out over the property, checking every nook and cranny for evidence. The coroner's truck was parked near the bay doors, and a single ambulance was close to it. He took a deep inhale of breath, then jumped from the driver's seat, slamming the car door closed behind him.

He hurried toward the interior of the building, flashing his badge as one patrol officer after another tried to stop him. As two body bags were carried out past him, Brennan felt himself begin to shake, his legs threatening to give out and send him to the floor. He took another breath and came to a standstill as he struggled to catch himself.

Cashel called his name, and when he looked up, his brother was standing at the entrance, waving him forward. "She's in here," he said.

As Cash turned, Brennan hurried after him. He still had no idea what he would find, and though he convinced himself he was prepared to face whatever, his confidence was completely shook.

EMS personnel hovered beside Stella. She lay on an ambulance stretcher, and when her hand moved, her fingers pushing at one of the technicians to leave her alone, Brennan released the breath he'd been holding.

"Is she okay?" he asked shooting a quick glance toward Cash.

"She's dehydrated and a little banged up, but they say she'll be fine. They had to give her a dose of Narcan to get her breathing again though. It seems Pamela gave them all an overdose of opioids. The brothers didn't make it."

Brennan could only begin to fathom what Stella had been made to go through as he glanced around the room. He and Cash exchanged one last look as the twins slapped palms. Brennan pushed his way to Stella's side. He leaned to wrap an arm above her head. His other grabbed her hand and kissed the back of her fingers. Her eyes were closed, and tears had dried against her cheeks.

"Hey, you still mad?" Brennan whispered into her ear.

Stella's eyes opened and she smiled. "Are you?" she whispered back.

"Yeah!" he said. "I'm mad as hell!"

"Me too!" She pressed her hand to his cheek, drawing the pad of her thumb along his profile. "I was so scared," she said. "Pamela has some serious issues! You need to catch her. It was a game, Brennan! A sick, evil game!"

He smiled. "She's already in custody. So is Tobias."

"But her boyfriend was…" she started to say.

Brennan shook his head. He leaned to press his lips to hers, kissing her ever so gently. "Shh! Don't let it worry you. We have it all under control. Let's get you home and healthy, and then I'll catch you up on everything you missed."

Stella lifted ever so slightly to kiss him a second time. "I have to tell you something," she said, shifting against the pillows behind her head.

He shook his head, tapping her lips with his index finger. "You just rest. I'm not going anywhere. I promise, you're going to have a really hard time getting rid of me."

Stella smiled. "I love you too," she said, and then she slowly drifted off to sleep.

* * *

When Stella was headed toward the hospital, Brennan moved to the other side of the room to catch up with Cash. "What'd you find?" he asked, his brother dictating instructions.

"We hit gold! Their entire lives were stored here in this warehouse. And Pamela kept meticulous records of every kill. Some go back ten years or more."

"Unreal!"

"And they collected trophies from their victims. We can tie them to the murders, and the DA should have no problems getting a conviction," Cash said with a nod. "That's one more down and many more to go. Our work never ends, but a win like this sure makes what we do worth it."

"Yeah," Brennan said, "but I like it so much better when the universe just drops them into our lap."

"Well, this case was clearly a slam dunk. I don't think any of us anticipated this outcome." Cash led him to the makeshift office area. There was a toaster oven and hot plate that sat on the surrounding counter. Someone had a real liking for strawberry Pop-Tarts and Little Debbie honey buns. Boxes of them had been stored in a cupboard over the counter. Bottled water was stacked in one corner. Paper littered the floor.

Cash passed him a pair of latex gloves, wanting to preserve as much of the evidence as they could. They were already battling layers of aged dust and dirt. The composition notebook was labeled with a woman's name. When you flipped open the cover, an image of the victim had been glued to the inside. Meticulous notes followed, weeks and months of surveillance until everything about that person had been discovered. Then came the plot to kill them. The how and why. Plans changed as every single solitary detail was weighed and measured. But every correction had been duly noted in pen and ink, sometimes accompanied by little scrolls and arrows.

It was bizarre in a way that gave Brennan pause. Surprisingly, it felt exactly like Pamela: disturbingly happy and joyful, and morbid in the same breath. She was proud of each project, wanting to commemorate that person's death with a yearbook of sorts. That last rah in their hurrah.

Each notebook was dated and adorned with pretty stickers, and ribbons in assorted colors were tied in lofty bows to keep them closed. There had to be at least two dozen or so lined neatly on a shelf. Brennan shook his head. He rested the book in his hand back onto the table. As he turned, something caught his eye. One last notebook that hadn't been completed. On the cover, Stella's name had been printed in a delicate calligraphy.

Stella opened her eyes to find Brennan sound asleep in the medical recliner beside her bed. He had leaned himself back, and his head was rolled to the side. His mouth was open, and he snored. Loudly. It made her smile, and she imagined that it was the first decent night's rest that he'd gotten in some time. She was sure that knowing he was close by and she was safe had done wonders for her.

When she'd wakened earlier, she'd requested copies of the morning newspapers. Someone had obliged her with the *Times*, the *Daily News*, the *Tribune*, the *Post*, and of course, the *Wire*. She and the Coltons had made the front pages yet again. This time the family received well-deserved accolades for the work they'd done in bringing down a family of killers. The mayor had pledged to honor them for a job well done and had reminded the community that they were working as diligently to bring the Landmark Killer to justice.

Brennan snored ever so slightly, and it made her smile. They still had far to go with their relationship, but the prospect of having him in her life and never again letting go of what they shared was pure joy. She was excited to learn things she didn't yet know, and the thought of them growing together as they reached for mutual goals made her heart sing.

Stella would never again *not* fight for them when it got hard, she thought, and Brennan had pledged the same to her. With a deep sigh, she closed her eyes and drifted back into the sweetest sleep.

"Stella!" Brennan called her name for the umpteenth time standing at the bottom of the stairs in her Harlem brownstone.

"I'm coming!" Stella yelled back. "Just give me one more minute!"

He shook his head. From the living room sofa, Rory and Cash both laughed at him.

"Leave that woman alone," Cash said. "She knows we're here."

"Yes, I do," Stella said as she bounded down the stairwell. "And your brother knows I was not dressed for company."

"You weren't dressed," Brennan said as he pressed a damp kiss to her lips.

She kissed his back, then turned away as she pulled the length of her dark hair into a ponytail that hung down her back. "Good morning, family," she said, moving to hug Rory first and then Cash.

"Good morning," Rory said with a laugh. "How are you doing?"

It had been three weeks since the FBI had found her left for dead in a local warehouse. She'd spent a few days in the hospital, then had come home to complete her recuperation. Brennan had been by her side the entire time, taking a short leave of absence from his responsibilities at the agency.

They had needed that time to recover and rebuild, working through those issues that had initially gotten in the way of a happily ever after. There had been some tears and a host of apologies and plans to prepare them for moving forward.

Brennan had jumped the gun talking about marriage, but Stella had slowed that propeller down to lots of dinner dates and the two of them living together. Neither of them were ready to say, "I do," without navigating what they did and didn't like about each other. Past experience had taught them both that love didn't necessarily fix all evil. That sometimes compromise and regret needed to coexist for a successful union. There were lessons that both needed to learn.

Today was going to be Brennan's first day back to work, leaving her alone. He was acting like a parent sending his child off to kindergarten for the first day of school.

"I'm fine," Stella said. She took a seat on the sofa. "I'm looking forward to getting some work done without nosy ears all up in my business." She shot Brennan a look.

"Aww," Cash said facetiously. "That's so cute!"

They all laughed warmly.

"I should be asking how things are going with you," Stella said. "Brennan told me you received another text message." She shot him a look, and he shrugged his shoulders.

"Yeah," Cash said. "It came to me this time. I swear, when we find who's sending these messages, I am going to hurt them. I'm going to hurt them bad."

Brennan narrowed his gaze on his brother. That anonymous text message had hit them all the wrong way and Cash was still raging over it. This time, the sender had mentioned Cashel's ex-wife. No worries. Lots where that dippy actor came from. Tsk-tsk, Cash—murdered Daddy and a sad ex-wife.

"We're really going to have to do something about your anger management issues," Brennan said.

"This coming from a man who threatened your boss with a fifteen-year prison sentence," Cash said, the comment directed at Stella.

Her eyes widened, shock and awe painting her expression. "You what? When did you do that?"

Rory laughed. "I keep telling you both, communication is the key to a good relationship."

Cash shook his head, continuing his thought. "Yeah, well, I tried communicating. After I got that text, I was worried about her. So I called to make sure she was okay. She was not interested in hearing from me, and she hung the phone up in my ear. I asked my buddy from the local precinct there on Coney Island to check up on her, maybe do a drive by or two at her high-rise."

Stella was still eyeing Brennan for an answer.

"We'll talk about it later," Brennan said as he moved to give Stella another kiss. "We have to go."

She kissed him again, pausing to wrap her arms around his neck as he hugged her back. "Be safe," she whispered.

Brennan nodded.

As the trio moved toward the home's front door, Rory's cell phone chimed. She paused to answer it, her face falling into deep thought. Her head was bobbing up and down. "We're on our way," she said as she disconnected the call.

"What's up," Brennan questioned, knowing the look she was giving them.

"We have another body. The Landmark Killer hit the Fondley Theater on Broadway late last night. He killed the assistant director of the play being performed there. A man named Viggo Olsen."

"Viggo?" Cash repeated. "Are they certain it's our guy?"

She nodded. "That's our V in Maeve. The note in his pocket confirms it's the Landmark Killer."

Brennan swore, the profanity punctuating her statement.

Stella followed them to the door. As Cash and Rory moved down the short flight of stairs, Brennan turned to kiss her one last time.

"It'll probably be a long night," he said. He slipped his arm around her waist and pulled her against him.

Stella kissed him back, her palms pressing against the hard lines of his chest. "I'll wait up for you," she said. "You'll probably need a little TLC when the day is over."

Brennan grinned and rushed out the door. He tossed one last glance over his shoulder, and Stella blew him a kiss. Both were past ready for their day to be done.

* * * * *

*For a sneak peek at the next
Coltons of New York story,*
Protecting Colton's Secret Daughters
by Lisa Childs, turn the page...

Chapter 1

Since the killings had begun, FBI special agent Cash Colton had spent more time at the Manhattan field office than he had anywhere else, so it felt strange to be outside now. Well, inside an SUV driving toward Coney Island, but it wasn't the office or a crime scene, which was the only other place he'd been besides the office.

At least Coney Island wasn't a crime scene yet. But after the text he'd received, the text that haunted him, Cash couldn't help fearing that he might be heading to another crime scene soon and not just because of the way that killer kept killing. That fear, because of that damn text, compelled him to make the trip to Coney Island, to make sure *she* was okay.

Even before receiving that text, he'd been as determined as the rest of his special unit to catch the Landmark Killer. The first victim, Mark Weldon, had been shot in Central Park and found with a typed note stuffed in his pocket: *Until the brilliant and beautiful Maeve O'Leary is freed, I will kill in her honor and name. M down, A up next.*

Like this guy could actually expect them to free a serial killer because of his threats? Then there would be two serial killers terrorizing New York, although Maeve hadn't limited her killing just to the Empire State. She'd killed wherever and whomever she'd married. She'd also tried to kill a lover's wife in order to inherit that woman's fortune. Anything for money...

Insatiable greed was Maeve's motive for murder.

Why was the Landmark Killer killing? What was his motive? Had Maeve somehow brainwashed him like she had that poor psychiatrist? Like she had all her husbands?

But even she had to see that there was no way she was getting released; she wasn't even going to get bail after the murders she'd committed.

That hadn't stopped her admirer, though. The Landmark Killer's second victim, Andrew Copowski, had been found on the Empire State Building observation deck with a typed note in his pocket. It had read nearly the same as the first, but the second line said, *MA down, E up.*

The next attempt had been on Broadway but that victim had fortunately survived. Unfortunately, since his assailant had worn a mask and a hoodie, he hadn't been able to provide much more than a vague description. Male, maybe on the younger side…

It wasn't much, but along with the other notes, not the ones left in the pockets of the victims but the personal texts the killer had sent, Cash and his team knew the killer was probably closer than they'd realized. Closer to them than they were to finding him.

He had to be stopped, before anyone else died, and before anyone else was threatened. Like Valentina had been threatened…

Maybe not specifically but the threat had been implied in the text Cash had received; he was the latest one singled out on the FBI serial-killer team. His twin had been the first to be taunted.

Who the hell was it? Was it someone close to them, like they had come to suspect? Someone within the FBI or within the 98th Precinct who had worked to hunt down the Black Widow serial killer, Maeve O'Leary? Someone who'd come to admire her for some sick reason?

The note about Valentina had been a text sent to Cash's phone after the first victim had been shot on Broadway. No worries. Lots where that dippy actor came from. Tsk-tsk, Cash—murdered Daddy and a sad ex-wife.

Instead of trying for another actor, the killer had claimed the life of an assistant theater director after that text. And what about Valentina?

Was she in danger? Had that text been meant as an actual threat or was it just a ploy to distract Cash from the case? While it likely was a ploy, Cash wasn't immune to the text. It had worked. He was distracted. He couldn't stop worrying about Valentina even though he'd told a friend at the local police precinct about the note and had asked Officer Dave Powers to watch out for her, to make sure that nobody was lurking around her, trying to hurt her.

Was she really sad?

Why?

She couldn't still be unhappy about their divorce. More than three years had passed since Cash had set her free to have what she'd really wanted: a husband who wasn't consumed with his work, and most especially children. More than anything else, more than him, Valentina had wanted a family.

Because Cash hadn't been able to see how he could handle his career, marriage and fatherhood, he'd done what he'd thought would make Valentina the happiest. After she'd moved out to get some space from him, he'd filed for divorce. He'd wanted her to have the happiness she deserved. So why wasn't she happy? Or was the texter lying about that?

He hadn't lied about Cash's murdered daddy. That had happened, and a serial killer was responsible for Cash's cop father losing his life.

And inadvertently responsible for Cash and all his siblings going into law enforcement.

So since he'd told the truth about that, he might have about Valentina as well. But how would the Landmark Killer know if Cash's ex-wife was happy or sad unless he'd gotten close to her? Did he know her? Or had he been stalking her like he had his victims?

Those worries kept Cash awake at night, kept him on edge. Even though he'd asked his buddy at the local precinct to keep an eye on her, Cash had also called Valentina to let her know about that text. To make sure she was aware of the potential threat. She'd been short with him, as if he'd caught her at a bad time. And maybe he had…

And ever since he'd heard her voice, he hadn't been able to get it out of his mind. Just as he'd never gotten Valentina Acosta completely out of his heart. Cash suspected that the Landmark Killer had known that when he'd sent Cash the text. He'd known how badly it would bother him, so somehow he knew Cash.

Maybe better than Cash knew himself because in the past three years he hadn't let himself admit to how he felt about Valentina. He rarely let himself think about her at all. If not for that damn text…

And then that call he'd made to her, to the same cell number she'd always had. Brennan had offered to make the call for him, as if it was somehow his fault that Cash had received the text even though their entire unit was hunting this sick serial killer. But he'd sent Brennan the first text: Shouldn't you be out looking for me, Agent Colton? Instead, you're shacking up with a murder suspect. I thought you Coltons didn't like killers since that one who got to your dear old daddy? I'm still out here, Agent. I'm headed to the theater. See you on Broadway!

Brennan had been reluctant to share the text with them. Probably because of the shacking-up part. Cash smiled and caught a glimpse of his own reflection in the rearview mirror. Despite being twins, he and Brennan looked nothing alike because they were fraternal, not identical. Brennan had pale blond hair and pale blue eyes and a baby face, while Cash had brown hair, green eyes and always looked like he needed a shave even if he'd just shaved. But given how busy he was, he'd given up and wore a beard now.

Valentina had always told him that she thought his scruff was sexy. But that was when he'd kept his beard nearly trimmed. He didn't look neat now. He probably should have stopped at home and showered after leaving the office, but for some reason he'd had this compulsion to drive to Brooklyn and Coney Island. To see for himself that Valentina was really all right, that she was safe and not sad.

"Valentina? Are you all right?"

The voice startled her, drawing her attention back to the present, and not the past, where it had been constantly slipping since that call a week ago. From Cash...

She had not heard the sound of his deep voice in three years, but she'd immediately recognized the rumble of it in her ear, goose bumps rising on her skin then like they were rising now despite the warmth of the library.

Valentina... he'd murmured.

"Valentina!" an older woman repeated again. "Are you all right?"

She shook her head and blinked and squinted against the late-afternoon sun pouring through the tall windows. Then she tried to focus on the woman standing in front of her, blocking her path, as Valentina had tried to push the double stroller between the rows of children's books.

"You're not all right," Mrs. Miller remarked, and she reached over the top of the stroller to pat Valentina's hand. "What's troubling you, honey?" The back of the woman's hand had thick veins crisscrossing it, and on every finger, below the swollen knuckle, she wore a ring with big stones that sparkled and reflected back the sunlight. The sun also glinted off the jewels hanging from the chains around her neck, too.

Four pudgy little hands stretched out from the stroller, reaching toward those shiny pendants. The girls loved shiny things.

Valentina smiled. "Nothing, Mrs. Miller. I'm fine. Really."

The woman stepped back then and leaned down to smile at the toddlers in the stroller. "How could you not be happy all the time with these two gorgeous girls?"

Mother's pride suffused Valentina. "I just picked them up from day care." If they didn't love going to school, as they called it, she might have regretted having to work full-time. But as a single mother, she didn't have a choice. At least she had a job that she enjoyed.

"And you came right back to work?" Mrs. Miller asked with surprise.

"We're picking out a book for bedtime. Well, two books. They each get to choose one."

"You're passing your librarian's love for books on

to your little girls—that's wonderful," Mrs. Miller enthused. "And speaking of books…"

"I tracked down that memoir you've been looking for," Valentina assured her.

"That's wonderful!" the woman exclaimed, her pale blue eyes sparkling like her rings with excitement.

"I ordered it to be sent here from the branch where I found it. If it arrives while I'm off this weekend, I asked Randall to call you and let you know if it gets here before Monday," Valentina said.

"I can wait until you're back on Monday, honey," the woman said. "Then you and I can discuss it."

That was one of the parts of Valentina's job that she enjoyed most. Discussing books with other avid readers.

The older woman loved reading the memoirs of famous theater actors and actresses and socialites and artists from years past, probably looking for a mention of herself. She'd once been an actress before marrying well and becoming a socialite; there was even a rumor that she had also been a famous artist's model and muse.

"When are you going to write your memoir?" Valentina asked. "Yours is the book I would love to read."

The older woman blushed and giggled and waved a hand in front of her face, and the sunlight glinted off all of the bright stones on her rings. She had that air about her, with the furs she wore and her perfect makeup and clothes and jewelry, of old Hollywood glamour. "I might be scribbling down a few notes here and there," she admitted with a sly smile. "But I find myself focusing on other things and events more than myself. I'm definitely not the type to kiss and tell. But I certainly enjoy reading the stories from the people who do."

Valentina laughed now, and the girls echoed it, despite having no idea what she was laughing about.

Mrs. Miller giggled again, and she looked much younger than her probably eighty or ninety years. "You enjoy your bedtime stories," she told them, and she patted Valentina's hand again as she walked past them.

The little girls leaned out either side of the stroller and stared after the older woman.

"Sparky…" Luciana murmured.

"Sparky," Ana repeated.

They must have been talking about the older woman's jewelry. Valentina smiled as her heart filled with love. They were so adorable with brown curls framing their little faces. Ana had dark eyes, like Valentina, while Luci's were green, like…

No. She wasn't going to think about him anymore. And for the next while, she managed that while helping the girls pick out books. But they knew the routine, so they chose quickly once they ruled out the ones they'd already read. Then they checked out and were back in the stroller, heading toward home, shortly after Mrs. Miller left.

The distance between the library and the high-rise condo complex where they lived was far enough that it was easier and safer to push the girls in their double stroller than for them to walk. The only problem was that with the street noise from traffic echoing off the commercial buildings, Valentina couldn't hear much of their chatter. Not that she understood much of it; they had their own little twin language. While they always understood each other, it wasn't as easy for Valentina all the time.

She still wasn't certain she understood Cash's call either. He'd received a text about her from a serial killer? Or so he and the rest of his unit suspected, but nobody at the FBI had been able to trace it. With all their technology, how was that possible?

And why send Cash a text about her?

She had not had any contact with her ex-husband since that day she'd moved out in order to take some time to think, to figure out if she could accept what he was willing to give her—whatever time that was left from the job that consumed him. But she'd wanted more than that; she'd wanted a family. And that was the one thing he'd told her he would not give her. But he actually had...

Neither of them had known it when she'd moved out, though. She hadn't even known it when the divorce papers had come. Thinking he didn't care enough to figure out a compromise with her, Valentina had just signed them and ended it without an argument, without a fight. And she'd thought it was done, that she would never see or hear from him again. And she hadn't for three years...

Until that night a week ago.

Valentina...

And just the sound of his deep, rumbly voice had

all the feelings rushing back, overwhelmingly intense. The pain, the loss, the guilt…

She should have told him all those years ago when she'd first found out herself that she was pregnant. But she'd figured that it was too late then because she had already signed the divorce papers. And in sending them, Cash had clearly been sending her the message that there was no hope for them as a couple. They were over. Done. He hadn't wanted the same things she had. He certainly hadn't wanted—

A loud pop rang out, startling her and making her jump. It wasn't so much the noise, which must have been a backfiring car that had passed by or started up along the curb or in one of the alleys they'd passed. It was that she'd been so distracted again that she hadn't even realized where she was. That she had almost walked past the street on which she needed to turn and cross to head home. She had to put that phone call out of her mind.

Cash hadn't called again. And he probably wouldn't. She knew he was busy chasing another killer, like he always was. The Landmark Killer. She'd watched the news and had read the article the *New York Wire* had recently run about the investigation.

No, that article had been more about the investigators than anything else. It had been all about the Coltons, who all worked in the elite serial-killer unit of the FBI. And it had revealed the reason why they were all on that unit and so dedicated to hunting down killers was that a serial killer had murdered their police officer father so many years ago.

But were they hunting the Landmark Killer, or was he hunting them with the notes he left in his victims' pockets and with the text he'd sent Cash?

She didn't know exactly what it had said, just that it had mentioned her. Since she and Cash had had no contact since their divorce, how had this serial killer known about her at all?

Was she in danger? And the girls?

Or were Cash and his siblings really the ones who were in danger and the serial killer was just texting to taunt them like he did with those notes he left on his victims?

He had killed again.

Like he had so many times before. That didn't even bother him anymore.

Taking a life.

It wasn't a big deal. It was just what he did, like other guys who played video games. But it wasn't a game to him. It was a vocation.

One he had to protect at all costs.

This time he couldn't be certain that he wouldn't get caught. He couldn't be certain unless he *made* certain. He had to eliminate any possibility of being identified as the killer.

So he settled into the driver's seat and pulled the mask over his face and drew up his hood, pulling it tight around that mask so that nothing of his face reflected back at him from the rearview mirror. Nothing but his eyes. His cold, dark eyes.

Chapter 2

Cash knew Valentina's address. She'd given it to him to forward her mail to after she'd moved out of the apartment they'd shared in Manhattan. She'd moved to Coney Island into the condo where her grandparents used to live. Her grandparents, knowing how much their only granddaughter had loved visiting them there, had left the condo to her in their will when they'd passed away shortly before Cash and Valentina's divorce. Valentina had wanted to move out there then, while Cash had wanted to stay close to the Manhattan office.

Maybe losing so much of her family had made Valentina even more desperate to start one of her own. That was when she'd really started pressuring Cash into having kids, and she'd wanted to raise her children in a place she remembered so fondly from her own childhood. Cash didn't have that many fond memories of his childhood; his father's brutal murder had overshadowed all of the happy ones.

It overshadowed his adulthood, leading him to a life in law enforcement. With his job consuming so much of his time and attention, he shouldn't have become a husband, let alone a father.

Valentina had often told him, during the three years that they'd been married, that she'd felt like a mistress and his career was really his wife. She only got stolen moments of his time, and he'd almost seemed guilty about the time he'd spent with her, the time away from his job. It hadn't been fair to Valentina. She shouldn't have been alone so much while he'd been working. She'd deserved so much more from their marriage, from him. She'd deserved everything she'd wanted.

She was so sweet and loving and smart and beautiful. So very beautiful…

He could see her now in his mind and maybe he even conjured up her image through the side window. Her thick dark hair flowing nearly to her waist, her hips swaying as she walked along the sidewalk. But she was pushing something in front of her. A stroller?

Was she babysitting for a friend?

Or had she started that family she'd wanted with him with someone else? That was what he'd hoped for her when he'd divorced her, but knowing that she had actually moved on with someone else…

And he hadn't. That he was still stuck in their past,

dreaming of her smile, of her laugh, of her wicked sense of humor flashing in her dark eyes, and the love…

A car horn tooted behind him and he realized the light had changed to green and the traffic in front of him had moved. But he was still stuck.

He pressed on the accelerator and surged forward through the intersection. The light green at the next one, he drove through that as well because he spied an open parking space ahead on the curb. He was nearly to her condo building. That had to be where she was heading. So he pulled into that spot and hopped out of his SUV. She would be coming this way if she was going home.

But maybe she'd been babysitting for someone and was taking the child back to their parents. Or was she the parent? Had she had the child she wanted? The family?

He wanted to be happy for her. But a part of him had never stopped wanting her…for her. And if that was her he'd seen on the sidewalk, she was every bit as beautiful as she'd always been. As sexy…

His heart pounded hard as he skirted around his SUV and stepped onto the sidewalk. He'd only gotten a couple of blocks ahead of her. She should appear soon, but the sidewalk was packed with people heading toward him, probably intent on enjoying the sunny day at the amusement park or the beach. And her complex was so close to both.

Instead of waiting for her to pass by him, Cash started through the crowd, moving against the throng of people. It had been three years since he'd seen Valentina; maybe that hadn't even been her he'd glimpsed on the sidewalk. Maybe that woman just looked like Valentina with the same curves and the same walk.

But if that woman wasn't his ex-wife, he doubted his heart would be pounding as fast and hard as it was. It wasn't just attraction or anticipation coursing through him, though; it was fear. Something had compelled him to drive out to Coney Island today to make sure she was safe. He'd been worried since he'd received that text, but that worry had intensified, twisting his guts, because he had a sick feeling, almost a premonition, that she was in danger.

He moved faster through the crowd, drawing grunts and curses as he accidentally banged into people. Maybe if they hadn't been on their phones and distracted they would have seen him coming, but he grunted back apologies. Until he neared the next intersection and he saw *her* standing on the other side, then he was the one distracted.

The woman was definitely Valentina. She stood at the curb in front of that stroller, although she was half turned toward it, her hand on top of it as if she was protecting it from the traffic on the street in front of her. The breeze coming in off the ocean played with her hair, swirling the long chocolate-brown tresses around her while plastering her light blue cotton dress against her curves. He knew that body so well that his body tightened with the desire coursing through him. He'd never wanted anyone the way he'd wanted her.

The way he still wanted her...

She didn't see him. Her focus was split between the stroller and the crosswalk light. Once it turned green, she held back a moment, letting other people pass by her. Then, finally, she started across, and just as she did, Cash heard an engine rev, brakes squeal and metal scrape as a car sideswiped the one stopped in front of it to pass it and roar toward the intersection, toward Valentina and that stroller with not one but two children in it.

His heart slammed against his ribs as fear shot through him. He'd been right to worry about her; she was definitely in danger.

Mortal danger...

The asphalt was hard and hot beneath her back. The impact with which Valentina had struck the ground had knocked the breath from her lungs, and she couldn't get it back, not with the heavy weight lying on top of her, pressing her into the ground. Panic gripped her, and now her lungs burned with a scream as well as her lack of breath.

The kids!

The stroller. Had it been knocked over as well? Or had the car done that?

It wasn't the car lying atop Valentina; it was a long, hard body. A familiar body that, even now, after three years, she recognized the feel of it pressed against hers. Instead of savoring the sensation, Valentina shoved at his shoulders, pushing him off. She had to find her babies.

Their babies...

The stroller was still upright, but the girls were crying and reaching out toward her. Fortunately they were strapped in, and while they were scared, they didn't appear harmed. Tears streaked out of Valentina's eyes.

Cash, who'd rolled off her, vaulted to his feet and helped her up. "Are you all right?"

She didn't care about herself; she ran toward her children to check on them. Make sure they were okay. No scratches. No bumps or bruises. So, thank God, the car hadn't struck the stroller at all. Cash must have shoved it out of the way when he'd knocked her down.

"It's okay, it's okay," she murmured to them. Then she turned back toward Cash and asked, "What happened?"

"A black car nearly ran us down," Cash said, but he was speaking into his cell phone, reciting a plate number that he must have somehow been able to read. He wasn't even looking at her. Or the kids.

She didn't want him to; she didn't want him to see her and definitely didn't want him to get a good look at the girls. Most of all, she didn't want to have to explain what she'd done and why she'd kept the secret for so long.

Right now, she just wanted to get herself and her daughters safely away from there, far from that car and ever farther from Cash.

But as she reached for the handle of the stroller, she heard the deep rev of an engine again and the squeal of tires. And she turned and saw that the black car had started back toward them…

* * *

Damn it!

How the hell had he missed?

He'd been so close. Too close to give up so soon. No matter that people had called 9-1-1; the police wouldn't get there for a few minutes. So he turned around at the next intersection, scraping cars that were parked along the curb as he made a sharp U-turn to once again face that intersection.

The woman was standing again, right in the middle of the street, next to that big stroller.

Totally focused on his target, he pressed hard on the accelerator and headed straight toward them.

This time he would not miss.

HARLEQUIN
PLUS

Try the best multimedia
subscription service for romance
readers like you!

Read, Watch and Play.

Experience the easiest way to get
the romance content you crave.

Start your **FREE TRIAL** at
<u>www.harlequinplus.com/freetrial</u>.